This book has been
donated by the Friends of
the Lake County Library
for the 2009 Be Creative
Summer Reading
Program.

JEMMA HARTMAN,
camper extraordinaire

Also by Brenda A. Ferber

Julia's Kitchen

JEMMA HARTMAN,
camper extraordinaire

Brenda A. Ferber

FARRAR, STRAUS AND GIROUX
NEW YORK

For Faith Ferber, daughter extraordinaire

The author gratefully acknowledges Dr. R. Scott Schappe,
Associate Professor and Chair, Department of Physics,
Lake Forest College, Lake Forest, Illinois, for his close, critical reading
of all material pertaining to sailing.

Copyright © 2009 by Brenda A. Ferber
Map copyright © 2009 by Jonathan Bartlett
All rights reserved
Distributed in Canada by Douglas & McIntyre Ltd.
Printed in the United States of America
Designed by Jonathan Bartlett
First edition, 2009
1   3   5   7   9   10   8   6   4   2

www.fsgkidsbooks.com

Library of Congress Cataloging-in-Publication Data
Ferber, Brenda A.
   Jemma Hartman, camper extraordinaire / Brenda A. Ferber.— 1st ed.
       p.   cm.
   Summary: Spending the summer after fifth grade at Camp Star Lake in
Wisconsin, Jemma discovers the joy of sailing and learns a lesson about
friendship.
   ISBN-13: 978-0-374-33672-1
   ISBN-10: 0-374-33672-5
   [1. Camps—Fiction.   2. Best friends—Fiction.   3. Friendship—Fiction.
4. Sailing—Fiction.]   I. Title.

PZ7.F3543 Je 2009
[Fic]—dc22

                                                              2008026049

You can't control the wind, but you can adjust your sail.
—*Anonymous*

JEMMA HARTMAN,
camper extraordinaire

1

Tammy said we'd be best friends forever, and I believed her. I was standing on her driveway, squinting in the August sun. The moving truck had left, and Tammy's parents and older brother were already in their minivan. Tammy and I did our secret handshake, complete with butt bump and shimmy. We hugged and promised to call. Then Tammy climbed into the van, and they drove away. The Eriksons were moving to Chicago, only thirty minutes by car from our life here in Deerfield. But when you were about to start fifth grade, anything farther than a bike ride was another world.

Now, finally, eleven long months later, we were going to reunite. I marked a big red X through July 15 on my wall calendar. Tomorrow morning Tammy and I were heading to Camp Star Lake for Girls in northern Wisconsin. Together.

I stepped around the two lumpy duffel bags taking up most of the floor in my bedroom, hopped onto my bed, and looked at my list of things to remember for the bus.

Toothbrush
Hairbrush
Pillow
~~Henry Henry~~ Henry!

I rubbed the worn-off spot on my stuffed dog's nose. It would be fine to take him. On the packing information sheet, the camp said to bring a "bedtime buddy." Tammy would probably take her baby blanket, and that was even rattier than Henry. If only she would return my calls or answer my IMs so I could be sure. Tammy had been impossible to get ahold of these last two weeks. Tonight her away message said, *packin for csl . . . leavin in the morn . . . one month w/ no computer! ahhh!!!!* At least tomorrow I wouldn't have to rely on technology to talk to her.

Even though I'd practically memorized the whole camp brochure, I took it out and studied it again. My favorite picture was of two girls laughing together in a little sailboat with a red, orange, and yellow sail. One of the girls had long blond hair, like Tammy, and the other

4

had straight brown hair, like me. I always imagined it was us in the boat. And riding the horses. And water-skiing. And with all those girls singing around a camp-fire.

I snuggled under the covers but didn't feel the tiniest bit sleepy. Even the sound of Snowball, my brother Derek's hamster, tap, tap, tapping on his wheel on the other side of the wall didn't calm me the way it normally did. Instead, my mind was racing as fast as his tiny feet. I hoped camp would be every bit as awesome as I'd imagined.

I listened to Mom and Dad turn on the dishwasher, turn off the lights, and head toward my room. They came in and gave me an extra-long sandwich hug. Mom smelled like fabric softener, and Dad like a Hershey's Kiss. It was a good thing Derek was too young to go to overnight camp. Otherwise Mom and Dad would be really lonely this summer. "Don't worry," I told them. "You're going to be okay without me."

They laughed, and Dad said, "We'll try to survive."

Mom took off my glasses and put them on the end table. "I'm not going to be there to remind you to take these off at camp, you know," she said.

"Well, maybe I'll leave them on so I can see my dreams better."

Mom and Dad smiled, and Dad said, "We're going to miss you, Jem."

"I'll miss you, too." With a pang in my heart, I realized that was true. "One more hug," I said, and they both squeezed me tight.

After they went to their own room, I still wasn't sleepy, so I got out of bed, put on my glasses, and looked out my window. The moon was a bright half circle in the sky. It was hard to believe I'd be looking at the same moon from the northern tip of Wisconsin tomorrow night. I wondered if it would look any different. I knew the quicker I went to sleep, the quicker I'd wake up and have this adventure begin. But right then I felt the way I did on roller coasters. I loved scary rides—the faster the better. But I hated that sensation at the top of the first big hill, when you knew there was no turning back.

I searched the night sky until I found a star. Then I closed my eyes and whispered, "I wish that Tammy and I have the best summer ever." I opened my eyes and looked at the star again. It seemed to be moving. Maybe it was a shooting star! No, it wasn't a star at all. It was an airplane.

• • •

The next morning, in the parking lot of the Strike-n-Spare bowling alley, I climbed aboard one of the two chartered buses and saw that girls were saving spots, and that the seats were filling up fast. I tossed my backpack and pillow across a pair of seats in the middle of the bus. I figured that was the best position, not too close to the driver, and not too near the bathroom.

Then I headed back out to the parking lot to join my family and wait for Tammy. We were supposed to leave in ten minutes, and she still hadn't arrived.

"Where can she be?" I asked Mom.

"Probably just stuck in traffic."

"What if she misses the bus?" Derek asked.

Dad shot Derek a look and draped his arm over my shoulder. "Don't worry, Jem. They won't leave without her."

I took a deep breath and scanned the crowd again. The parking lot was a mishmash of cars and families, parents drinking coffee and taking pictures, kids squealing and hugging each other, and other kids, first-timers like me, standing uneasily with their parents. One of those girls, a tall, skinny one with frizzy brown hair, waved shyly at me. I started to wave back when an older girl with beautiful long dark curls grabbed her attention. I was in mid-wave, wondering if maybe she hadn't meant to wave to me in the first place, so I pretended to swipe a gnat from my face.

I pushed my glasses up on my nose. The back of my neck was sweaty, so I pulled my hair up into a ponytail. Then I untied and tied my gym shoes, trying to look busy.

Finally the Eriksons' minivan pulled into the parking lot, and relief rushed through me. "She's here!" I jumped up and down and weaved my way over to Tammy's minivan.

The door slid open, and Tammy stepped out, wearing a handmade I ♥ CAMP STAR LAKE shirt and sporting a short new hairstyle that caught me by surprise. We screamed and hugged each other, and then I asked, "What happened to your hair?"

"I donated it to Locks of Love," she said. "You know, for kids who lose their hair from cancer and stuff. Do you like it?"

"It's cute," I said. "Perky." I thought about my own hair and suddenly felt guilty for keeping it to myself. Maybe I'd donate it, too.

Tammy stepped aside as another girl came out of the minivan. "You remember my cousin Brooke, right?"

Brooke was wearing a shirt just like Tammy's. She had straight, shiny brown hair, blue eyes, and freckles sprinkled across her nose and cheeks. "You're Brooke, from California?" I asked.

She nodded. "The one and only."

I shifted my weight from one foot to the other, wondering why Brooke was here and why she and Tammy were dressed like twins. "Too bad you're visiting when Tammy's leaving for camp."

Brooke raised her eyebrows at me and gave Tammy a sideways glance.

Tammy said, "Oh my God! I forgot to tell you. Brooke is coming to camp, too. Isn't that great?"

Huh? I was too shocked to think, let alone say anything, but I didn't have a chance to, anyway. Tammy's parents and Brooke's mom were asking them to help with the duffels. My family came up behind me just as Mrs. Erikson shut the trunk, and Tammy and Brooke hurried off with their parents to check in with Eddie Kramer, Camp Star Lake's director.

"Who's that girl?" Derek asked.

"That's Tammy's cousin Brooke. She's coming to camp, too." My voice sounded so normal, which was strange because that was not at all how I felt.

"Really?" Mom said, and I could tell by her face that she was as surprised as I was. "Well, the more the merrier, right?"

Eddie blew a whistle and spoke into a megaphone. "Time to go, girls. Say your goodbyes, and let's hit the road!"

My stomach dropped. *Whoosh*. The roller coaster was speeding downhill. And all I could do was hold on tight.

2

I boarded the bus with Tammy and Brooke, and as we walked down the aisle, I suddenly realized there was a problem. "Shoot, Brooke. I only saved these two seats. Sorry."

"Oh," Brooke said. "Well . . ." She looked at Tammy. But what could Tammy do? All the seats near us were taken.

"Maybe we can all three squish in," I offered.

Brooke scrunched her face and said, "For seven hours?" The left side of her upper lip rose in a look of disgust, and she peered down her nose at me.

Alarm bells went off in my head. Should I have seen into the future and saved three seats instead of two? "I'm just trying to include you," I explained.

Brooke narrowed her eyes at me, and I felt as

though I'd once again said the wrong thing. Didn't Brooke know that Tammy and I were best friends? Tammy smiled weakly at me, then peered around at the seats near us—the seats that were all taken. Some girls attempted to pass us in the aisle.

"Jemma," Tammy said, and she stared at me as if trying to communicate via ESP, but the message didn't come through. Then she motioned for me to follow her. We left Brooke at our seats and walked down the aisle to the back of the bus.

Tammy stood against the bathroom door and tugged on her earlobe, a habit I'd seen since kindergarten. Tammy's face had gotten thinner. Her chubby cheeks had disappeared. And her new short hair made her eyes, which were the golden brown of perfectly toasted marshmallows, seem larger. She was prettier than before, older-looking. She had even begun to develop curves. I was still flat as a second grader, but I wondered if I seemed any different to her.

She leaned in so only I could hear her, and she said, "Brooke's parents are getting divorced. *And* she and her mom are moving. *And* she just found out about all this two weeks ago."

"Oh man, that stinks."

"Seriously. So she's having a hard time, and I kind of need to take care of her. So . . . do you mind if I sit with her?"

My stomach knotted. I knew I should sympathize

with poor Brooke and admire Tammy's sense of caring and duty. And I should be happy to let Tammy sit with Brooke. But that was not how I felt. I did mind!

Tammy lifted her shoulders and tilted her head to the side with a hopeful look on her face. I took a deep breath. I didn't want to let Tammy down. I didn't want to start camp off on the wrong foot. Besides, it was just a bus ride. "No problem," I said. "We'll eat together at lunch."

"Jemma, you're the best." Tammy smiled and hugged me, and I was proud of myself even though the knot in my stomach did not disappear. I had done the nice thing, the thing Tammy would have done if the tables had been turned, but still, something was wrong.

Tammy hurried back up to the seats I'd saved. I followed behind, grabbed my backpack and pillow, and found the only seat left on the bus—squished in the back between a first-aid kit and the stinky bathroom.

As the bus pulled out of the parking lot, I waved to Mom, Dad, and Derek, but they didn't see me through the tinted windows. I was sure of that because they were waving to a girl about ten rows in front of me. Oh well. It was better to pretend to wave goodbye to my family than to sit there all alone, like a nobody.

Once we'd gotten onto the highway, Tammy ran down the aisle and said, "I almost forgot. I made you a shirt!" She tossed the shirt my way before a counselor told her to get back to her seat. I unfolded the white cotton T and saw another I ♥ CAMP STAR LAKE design. I brought the shirt right up to my nose and breathed in the cotton and fabric paint before pulling it on over my plain yellow tank top. Even though my best friend was sitting with her cousin, and I was sitting next to the bathroom, I knew I hadn't been completely forgotten.

We sang songs while the bus rolled out of Illinois and into Wisconsin. I learned the Camp Star Lake song. And for the first time in my life, I sang "One Hundred Bottles of Beer on the Wall" and actually made it to zero. I stared out the window as we passed farms and cornfields. I didn't know what to make of Brooke's being here. I'd known all along that there would be other girls at camp besides Tammy and me. So why did I care? Maybe Mom was right. The more the merrier, I told myself.

Sitting in front of me were two girls who seemed to be identical twins. They both had red hair and looked about my age. One of them snorted every time she laughed. The other one was constantly patting out a rhythm on her legs. Through the crack between the seats, I watched them dig into a bag of Starburst jelly beans. After what felt like hours later, the snorting girl turned around, kneeled in her seat, and asked, "Do you like yellows?" She held out a handful.

"Sure," I said. "Thanks."

"I'm Kat O'Reilly," she said. "And you're new. Star Lake is small enough to know everyone, and this is our second year here. I would definitely know you otherwise, so welcome!"

Kat talked so quickly and with so much energy, I couldn't help but smile. The other girl poked her head up over the seat and removed her iPod earbuds. "Hi," she said.

"That's Annie," Kat said. "We're twins, and yes, we're identical—everyone always asks."

Red hair. Black eyebrows. Brown eyes. Quite an interesting combination, especially when there were two of them. Kat was wearing a necklace with a silver *K* on it. Annie had one with an *A*. "I'm Jemma," I said.

"Jenna?" Kat asked.

"No, Jemma, with an *m*." Sometimes it felt like "with an *m*" was my middle name. Jemma With-an-*m* Hartman.

"Cool," Kat said. "I'm Kat with a *K*."

I liked this Kat with a *K*. I could tell she was the kind of person Tammy and I would get along with.

"You're going to love CSL," Kat and Annie both said at once. Then they looked at each other and laughed.

"Do you guys always do that?" It was kind of freaky, but cool, watching them talk at the same time with the same facial expressions.

"Sometimes," they said together again.

We all laughed then. I ate the jelly beans, and Kat and Annie told me they were going into sixth grade, too. They said there were usually only two cabins of sixth graders, so we had a good chance to be together. I tried to point Tammy out to them, but she was too far forward for them to see. "Which activities are you going to take?" I asked.

Kat said, "We spend most of our day in the gym. We take every dance class they offer, like jazz, ballet, tap, hip-hop. Oh, and acrobatics and gymnastics, too."

"Kat's a great dancer," Annie said.

"So is Annie."

Annie crinkled her nose and shook her head to let me know she didn't agree.

"Last year they didn't have break dancing, but Annie and I begged Eddie to add it this year, so I guess we'll find out tonight." The whole time Kat was talking, Annie was nodding and tapping her fingers on the top of the seat back as if she had a song going through her head, even though her iPod was off. "What about you?" Kat asked. "Do you dance?"

"Not really. I'm more into sports."

For a second, I wondered if I was insulting them by not liking dance, but Kat said, "Well, that's what's so great about CSL. You get to take the classes that interest you."

"Unless you have a twin sister who makes you take all the same classes as her," Annie said.

Kat playfully elbowed Annie. "So not true! You know we just like the same things."

Annie shrugged and raised her eyebrows. Kat

seemed to think Annie was kidding. Maybe she was. Kat tilted the jelly bean bag my way, and I took some more. "And the sports here are awesome, too, especially the water sports. Waterskiing, swimming, sailing . . ."

"Yeah, I can't wait to learn to sail!" I thought again about being in that pretty boat with Tammy. Just the two of us. "So what else should I know?"

They both asked, "What do you want to know?" Then Kat did her snorty laugh.

I smiled and said, "Tell me about that award . . . Firelighter." I had read in the brochure about Fireside, camp's Sunday evening program, and about Firelighter. There was a picture of a girl holding a torch in front of a big bonfire. She was smiling so wide I thought her face might split, and her eyes glistened with what I could only guess were happy tears. The brochure said the Firelighter was a camp role model, "someone who embodies the character and spirit of Camp Star Lake."

"How do you win it?" I asked.

Kat and Annie looked at each other quickly; then they both shook their heads. Kat said, "No no no. You don't *win* Firelighter. You earn it."

I wasn't sure what the difference was, but I didn't want to sound like an idiot. "Okay, then. How do you earn it?" My question was directed to Kat, who seemed to do most of the talking for these two.

Kat whispered as if she was letting me in on an important secret. "For one thing, you don't ask questions like that because you don't want anyone to think you're trying to be Firelighter."

I was more confused than ever. "Why wouldn't I try to be Firelighter? It's a cool award, right? Why wouldn't everyone try?"

"It is cool. The coolest. But you just can't. Either you're Firelighter material or you're not, and Eddie spots the phonies a mile away."

"Everyone does," Annie added, and her fingers seemed to tap an exclamation mark on the seat back.

Kat said, "There was this one girl last year—"

"Vanessa!" Annie made a face as if she were going to barf.

"Yes. Vanessa was the meanest girl ever, but if a counselor or Eddie happened to be nearby, she would all of a sudden turn into Miss Sweet Helpful Camper, just bursting with camp spirit."

"It was disgusting," Annie said, picking three purple jelly beans out of the bag and popping them into her mouth.

"So did she get to be the Firelighter?" I asked.

"No!" they both said, a little too loudly. So much for me not sounding like an idiot.

"That's the point," Kat said. "Everyone knew she was *trying* to be Firelighter."

"Oh," I said, as if it all made sense to me. And it sort of did. To be the Firelighter, you not only had to embody the character and spirit of Camp Star Lake—

whatever that meant—but you also had to act like it was the last thing on your mind. I wondered if I could do that. I wondered if Tammy could. Maybe Tammy and I could be Firelighters together. "Were you guys ever Firelighters?"

"No," Kat said. "First-year campers almost never get it. It's usually the girls from Woods. That's the oldest cabin."

That didn't seem very fair to me. I wanted to ask Kat and Annie more questions about Star Lake. They seemed to know things the brochure could never tell me. But we were pulling into McDonald's, and that meant it was time for lunch with Tammy. Yes!

3

I joined Tammy and Brooke in a booth by the window. Brooke unwrapped her straw halfway and blew the wrapper at Tammy's face. Tammy laughed and blew hers back at Brooke. Then I tried to blow mine at Tammy, but there was a hole in it.

"Hey, since when do you eat chicken nuggets?" I asked Tammy as I got ready to chow down on my Quarter Pounder. She always used to order the double cheeseburger.

Tammy shrugged and dunked a nugget in honey mustard. "I don't know. I think Lindsey got me into them."

Lindsey was one of Tammy's new friends. I was sure she'd made tons of friends at her private school this year, even though we'd never talked much about it.

"Oh my gosh," Brooke said. "Lindsey's boat is slammin' cool."

Slammin'? Was that a California word? And why did Brooke know about Lindsey's boat when I didn't?

Tammy must have seen the questions on my face because she said, "Lindsey's parents have this amazing boat, and they took us out on Lake Michigan last week for a sunset sail."

"Fun!" I said. Then I turned to Brooke. "So, how long have you been visiting?"

"About two weeks." She sipped her Coke.

That explained why Tammy had been so unavailable lately.

"Actually," Tammy said, "Brooke and her mom are moving to Chicago, and they're staying with us until they find a place of their own."

"Really?" I dipped a French fry in ketchup and tried to keep my voice steady. I pictured Brooke sleeping in Tammy's trundle bed and staying up late at night the way we always did on our sleepovers. "Are you guys going to live near each other and go to the same school?" I held my breath as I waited for the answer.

"That's the plan," Tammy said.

No fair. No fair. No fair. "That's great," I squeaked.

"Yeah, it's funny," Tammy said. "We used to not even like each other that much, right, Brooke?"

Brooke laughed and nodded. "But that was because we barely spent any time together."

"Now we aren't just cousins. We're friends." Tammy reached across the table and squeezed Brooke's hand.

My throat closed up, and I choked down my fry. The more the merrier would never work if I was going to be the odd girl out. I wanted to find Eddie and tell him that Brooke had lice or some infectious disease and must be sent home immediately. I wanted to ask Tammy if she had any idea that I'd been missing her all year, and that she was now crushing my heart. But I didn't want Tammy to think I was insecure. They were just friends, not best friends. Brooke wasn't taking my place. So I tucked the ends of two fries between my gums and upper lip, like tusks. "Look," I said, "I'm a walrus."

Tammy laughed. But Brooke raised her lip as if she was disgusted, and when Tammy saw Brooke's reaction, her laughter crackled and died.

• • •

After lunch, back in my seat by the toilet, I watched the landscape fly by. Everything I'd imagined for the last six months had been focused on Tammy and me, reunited at camp. Now Brooke was in the picture, and all my dreams were out of whack. I was jealous. I knew I shouldn't be. But there it was, the ugly truth.

Even as I thought it, I knew it was ridiculous. I had nothing to be jealous of. Tammy was my best friend. We had a history. I was there when she peed in her pants in first grade rather than ask Ms. Wheeler, our scary gym teacher, for permission to go to the bathroom. She was the one who dared me to climb that tree in third grade, and she was also the one who ran yelling for help when I fell from it and broke my arm. I knew her favorite snacks were kettle corn and chocolate-covered pretzels. She knew I couldn't stand anything with raisins. We spied on her brother when he made out with Debby Lebold in the Eriksons' backyard. We carved our initials into the newly poured sidewalk in front of the library. We wrote a secret love song to our fourth-grade teacher, Mr. Bradley, then dropped it on his desk and pretended Tracy Silverman had done it. We made big plans. Life plans. Like rooming together in college. And marrying twin brothers. We even talked about living next door to each other someday so our kids could be best friends. I had no reason to be jealous of Brooke. No reason at all. If anything, she should be jealous of me.

I held on to this thought as we traveled north through Wisconsin. Tammy was just being a good cousin, helping Brooke through a rough spot. Everything would be fine.

I fell asleep for a bit, and when I woke up, the farms had disappeared and dark green forests had taken their place. Every once in a while, a shining blue lake appeared and broke up the endless stretch of trees.

All of a sudden, some girls pointed out the window and shouted, "White signs! White signs!"

I looked and saw a bunch of white arrow-shaped signs with black lettering on them. I didn't know what the big deal was, but the girls on the bus jumped up and down and cheered.

"What's going on?" I asked Kat.

"We're almost there!"

My heart raced, and I peered out the window as if I knew what I was looking for. Tall oaks, maples, and pine trees lined the road. Whenever we passed a new white sign, the excitement on the bus grew. The signs said EAGLE RIVER INN, BIRCHWOOD MOTEL, CAMP THUNDER RIDGE, and FULL MOON TAVERN.

Finally one of the little white signs said CAMP STAR LAKE, and everyone clapped and broke out in the camp song. Chills ran up and down my arms as I sang along. This was it! My summer at Camp Star Lake was about to begin.

We turned left onto a dirt road and passed between two stone pillars with painted wooden eagles perched on them. "The gooney birds!" Kat and Annie yelled, and everyone on the bus stood up. A sign next to one of the gooney birds said, "CAMP STAR LAKE FOR GIRLS. 59 SUMMERS OF FRIENDSHIP AND FUN." Dozens of counselors, all dressed in yellow and blue, clapped and cheered and ran alongside the buses. I tried to catch a glimpse of

Tammy, but there were too many girls between her and me.

We came to a stop in a grassy field in front of a building that looked like an oversized log cabin. Kat told me it was called the Lodge. It was two stories tall, with a wide porch encircling it and a thick stone chimney poking out of the roof. Everyone spilled out of the buses as fast as possible, but since my seat was next to the bathroom, I was the last one off. I stepped out into a sea of people. Campers and counselors were hugging. I guessed they must have known each other from prior summers. Kat and Annie ran off together. I looked for Tammy, but couldn't find her. I hoped nobody noticed how alone I was.

Eddie rang a big bell that stood on a post in front of the Lodge, and everyone quieted down. "Welcome to Camp Star Lake!" he said. "Who's ready for the best summer of their lives?" Everyone cheered, and I joined in. Sometimes you had to fake it till you could make it. Eventually Eddie held his hand high to quiet us down. "Listen up, and I'll read the cabin assignments. You girls have time to meet your counselors, unpack, and settle in before dinner."

Tammy and I had requested that we be in the same cabin, so I wasn't worried about that. I just wished I could find her in this mob. Eddie introduced the first counselor and read off the names of girls in her cabin.

Then he moved on to the next. As each group was announced, they set off for their cabin. And as the crowd thinned, I spotted Tammy, standing with Brooke. I ran over to them. "Hey, I was looking for you," I said, putting my arm around Tammy.

Tammy smiled widely and bumped hips with me. "And you found us! Oh my God, did you see the lake?" She pointed behind her, and I looked.

Whoa! The brochure didn't come close to capturing this beauty. We were standing on the top of a hill that led down to a sparkling blue lake. Trees lined the shore, and a few boats dotted the water. Off to the right were sports fields, with a horse-riding ring in the distance. The sky was blue, blue, blue, and the air smelled of pine and grass. Star Lake looked as though it was just waiting for us to jump right in. It didn't even matter that Brooke was here; I knew this summer would be amazing.

Eddie introduced a counselor with blond pigtails and blue and yellow ribbons in her hair. "This is Darby Coleman," he said. "She was a CSL camper for seven years and has been a counselor for three. One more year and we'll have to adopt her! This summer, she's in Cabin Six with Brooke Bernstein, Tammy Erikson, Jemma Hartman, Delaney Reed, Annie O'Reilly, and Kat O'Reilly." We all jumped up and cheered when our names were called. This time I didn't feel like I was faking at all. We dragged our duffels across the field and down the row of cabins until we came to Cabin Six. Darby held the screen door open, and we shuffled in.

I noticed two lightbulbs hanging from the ceiling and three bunk beds along the walls, but before I could take anything else in, there was a mad dash for the beds. Annie and Kat claimed the bunk closest to the door. Brooke jumped onto the bunk on the long wall and said, "This is for Tammy and me." Delaney, the tall, skinny girl with frizzy brown hair who sort of kind of maybe waved to me this morning, jumped onto the top of the last bunk, and I stood in the middle of the cabin, bewildered.

"Wait a minute," I said to Brooke, my heart tightening with anxiety. "Tammy and I were planning on bunking together."

But Brooke said, "No. I'm bunking with Tammy. That was our deal, right, Tam?"

I turned to Tammy, whose face was filled with guilt. We had talked about sharing a bunk way back in February. Had she forgotten? She bit her lower lip, then said, "Does it really matter, Jemma? I mean, we're just sleeping in these beds, right? Who cares who you're with when you're asleep?"

I felt Darby and the other girls looking at me. I knew people were trying to figure one another out, and I sure didn't want to be the camper everyone thought was a troublemaker. I wanted to be the one they said was Firelighter material, a camper extraordi-naire. Maybe Tammy had a point. It didn't matter all that much. "It's fine," I said. I forced a smile and put my backpack on the bunk below Delaney, who was wearing a shirt with the word BREATHE on it. Not such bad advice.

Darby said, "I'm glad you girls worked that out so nicely. That's what camp is all about—learning to get along with each other. Now, why don't you unpack, and we'll play a get-to-know-you game before dinner. I'll be in my room, which is right behind this door, if you need me. Oh, and the bathroom is around this corner."

As I unzipped my duffel, I couldn't help feeling the same way I did on the bus when I let Brooke have my seat. If I was doing the right thing, the good thing, how come I felt so bad?

Let's sit next to each other," I said to Tammy on the way to dinner.

She smiled and grabbed my hand. "Absolutely!" We walked like that all the way to the Lodge, and I felt normal again. This was how it was supposed to be: Tammy and me, chatting about everything and nothing—her brother's latest girlfriend, how cool Kat and Annie seemed, whether we thought we'd be homesick (no way!), the new Orlando Bloom movie, how weird it would be to have no computer or TV for four weeks . . .

Brooke was somewhere behind us. I didn't know exactly where, and I didn't even care. After unpacking, we'd played a game called Two Truths and a Lie. We'd each told two things about ourselves that were true and one that was a lie, and everyone had to guess which was the lie. I'd said, "My soccer team won the league championship this year. I live in a haunted house"—my lie. "And Tammy and I have been best friends since kindergarten."

Of course Brooke had to top me by saying, "My dog can talk. I know how to surf. And Tammy and I have been cousins since birth."

The Lodge was noisy with girls laughing and talking and wooden chairs scraping across the linoleum floor. I smelled barbecued chicken. "There's our table," I said, pointing to a round one with a Cabin Six sign on it. It was in the corner, right next to a wall of windows.

"What a view!" Tammy said. She sat down, and I sat next to her. Then she put her feet up on the chair on her other side and said, "I'll save this one for Brooke."

I looked out the window rather than acknowledge that. There was a water-skier trailing behind a speedboat in the middle of the lake. But no sailboats, as far as I could see. I took a deep breath.

"What are you doing?" Tammy asked, smirking. "Meditating?"

"Very funny." I elbowed her and laughed. In the truth-and-lie game, Delaney had said, "I've been practicing yoga since I was born. I meditate every day. And my favorite position is Happy Baby." None of us could guess which was her lie. I'd hoped they were all lies and she was just being funny. I'd rather have been bunkmates with a practical joker any day of the week than with a meditating yoga girl. But, no, Delaney was one hundred percent serious. It turned out that Happy Baby was her second favorite pose. Her favorite was something called Downward-Facing Dog. Okay. Whatever.

The rest of our cabinmates joined us, and Brooke whispered something in Tammy's ear. Tammy laughed. "What?" I said, but she just shook her head. I hoped Brooke wasn't whispering about me.

Darby came over and said, "Are you girls ready for Eddie's famous chicken?"

My stomach rumbled, I was so hungry.

"So here's how meals work at CSL." Darby pointed to a long table in the middle of the room. "All the counselors eat there. Eddie will call the cabins up one at a time to go through the cafeteria line. And when you're done eating, each of you clears your dishes, and one of you wipes the table. You girls will figure out a fair way to take turns, I'm sure. There are sponges up by the water pitchers." She put a pile of colorful envelopes on the table. "And believe it or not, you've already got mail!"

Kat grabbed the envelopes and started doling them out. Delaney raised her hand.

"Honey, you don't need to raise your hand here." Darby laughed gently.

Delaney licked her lips, which were dry and chapped. "Okay. But I just wanted to make sure there would be vegetarian offerings at all of our meals. My mom told me there would be."

Vegetarian offerings? My bunkmate was turning out

to be weirder and weirder. And her voice was so quiet, it was practically a whisper.

"You bet, sweetie. There's always a salad bar and peanut butter and jelly if you don't like what they're serving."

Kat slid a purple envelope my way. Even though I'd only been here for a couple of hours, I was excited to get mail. I ripped open my letter and read.

Dear Jemma,

It's strange to be writing to you now when you're in the family room watching TV. But I wanted to make sure you had a letter waiting for you when you got to camp. So, hi! I hope the bus ride wasn't too terrible. You and Tammy probably talked each other's ears off and made the time fly by.

Although you hardly complained this year, I know how much you missed Tammy, and Daddy and I are thrilled that you'll be able to have these four weeks with her at camp.

Write us soon and tell us about the girls in your cabin and all the fun activities you're doing.

Love you tons! xoxoxo, Mom

Reading Mom's letter made me realize how different things were than I'd expected. A lump grew in my throat, but I swallowed it down. If Mom were here right now, I'd tell her how Brooke was getting between Tammy and me, and Mom would hug me and tell me she was sorry things weren't going my way. Then she'd probably say I should imagine what it must be like for Brooke. Finding out your parents were getting divorced. Moving. Being shipped off to camp. I got it. I wouldn't want to be in Brooke's shoes. But still . . .

Annie tapped out a rhythm on the table. "Aren't you going to open yours?" she asked. I looked up and saw that she was talking to Brooke, who was turning a letter over in her hands. It was a plain white envelope addressed in small square handwriting. Tammy looked at the letter, then patted Brooke's back. Brooke placed the letter facedown on the table. I tried to read her expression, but I couldn't tell if she was sad or mad. I raised my eyebrows at Tammy, but she shook her head.

Why wasn't Brooke opening that letter? And who was it from? Maybe Tammy would explain later, when Brooke wasn't around.

• • •

After dinner we headed to the gym to create our schedules. We were allowed to choose five activities for Mondays, Wednesdays, and Fridays, and five more for

Tuesdays, Thursdays, and Saturdays. Every day there was an open period before dinner when we could go to any activity we wanted, and after dinner there was a cool evening program: CSL Beauty Pageant, Hawaiian Luau, Let's Make a Deal, even socials with neighboring boys' camps. Kat told us Eddie liked surprises. He would announce each evening's activity at lunchtime and not a minute sooner. On Sundays we would sleep late, then have a special all-camp event, like Pirate Day, Olympics, Gold Rush Day, or—Kat and Annie's favorite—Carnival. They loved the cotton candy. Sunday nights were for Fireside and the all-important Firelighter award.

Eddie's wife, Maureen, handed Tammy, Brooke, and me each a blank schedule that we could fill with our choices. Counselors sat behind long tables. On the wall above each counselor's head was a sign, starting with archery on the left and winding around the room alphabetically all the way to waterskiing on the right. There were already long lines at the waterskiing, tennis, and sailing tables.

"Let's sign up for sailing," I said to Tammy.

"Look at the line for waterskiing," Brooke said, taking a step closer to Tammy. "We better go there first, before all the classes fill up."

Tammy nodded, but I said, "They won't all fill up." This time I wanted to get my way, even if it was about something as dumb as which line to get into first.

"You never know," Brooke said to Tammy, as if Tammy had the final say—as if I didn't count at all. "We might not get to be in the same class if we wait."

I hadn't thought of that. And it made me want to get into the sailing line even more. Tammy and I just had to be together for sailing. "Well, we can't be in every class together, anyway," I said. I wondered if Brooke planned to be with Tammy and me every minute of every day here. If so, I'd go crazy. Tammy was standing between us, looking at the tables. I touched her elbow, and she met my gaze. "It makes more sense to be sure we're together for sailing. You do that with a partner." I hoped she knew that by partner I meant me.

Tammy said, "I don't really care, you guys. But while we're standing around arguing, every line is getting longer."

She was right about that. "So let's go," I said, pulling Tammy over to the sailing line and ending the argument for good. Brooke followed behind. One tiny victory for me.

We all ended up in the same sailing class, but by the time we got to the front of the waterskiing line, there weren't that many spots left. Darby was the counselor in charge, and she said, "Sorry, girls, I can't fit all three of you into one class. I can put two of you in first period Tuesday, Thursday, and Saturday, though."

"Me and Tammy!" Brooke and I both said at the same time.

Darby tilted her head at us. Her expression was a cross between amusement and pity.

Brooke put one hand on her hip and said to Tammy, "I told you the classes would fill up."

It was true, of course. But why did that matter? Did that mean she should get to be with Tammy? Brooke and I both looked at Tammy, waiting for her to choose. Tammy tugged on her earlobe. "Oh my God, you guys, this is so dumb . . ."

This wasn't dumb at all. This was important. Tammy should explain to Brooke that I was her best friend, that we'd been missing each other ever since she moved, that this was our summer to spend together, and that Brooke was going to have to deal with that.

I waited for her to say something. But she just stood there pulling on her ear. She probably didn't want to hurt either of us, so I decided to help her with a little logic. "You and Brooke sat together on the bus, and you're bunking together, so it's only fair that I get to be in skiing with you."

Brooke huffed out a breath, then narrowed her eyes and raised her lip at me again. I felt like a piece of chewed-up gum on the bottom of her shoe. Tammy squeezed Brooke's shoulder to comfort her. It seemed that once again Brooke was going to get her way.

But then suddenly Tammy lit up as if she had found the perfect answer. "I know! You guys should be in that class together. I don't mind, and it'll give you a chance to get to know each other better."

Darby grinned and nodded at Tammy. "Great idea," she said.

I couldn't have disagreed more. And if I was reading Brooke's face correctly, it seemed that finally she and I agreed.

5

At bedtime that night, we all compared our schedules. I liked the way mine turned out:

	Mon., Wed., Fri.	Tues., Thurs., Sat.
1st period	Soccer	Waterskiing
2nd period	Tennis	Ranching
3rd period	Gymnastics	Swimming
	Lunch/Rest	Lunch/Rest
4th period	Sailing	Horseback Riding
5th period	Basketball	Arts and Crafts

After the waterskiing dilemma, Darby had suggested that Tammy, Brooke, and I split up and choose our own activities, since we'd be spending plenty of time together, anyway. I ended up being with Tammy for ranching (where we'd get to take care of animals in the camp's mini-farm) and sailing. It was only two classes, but at least they were on different days.

Kat and Annie's schedules were almost exactly the same.

"Identical schedules, identical twins. What if you lose your necklaces?" Brooke asked. "How are we supposed to tell you apart?" Tammy, Delaney, and I crowded around Kat and Annie's bunk.

"Our schedules aren't identical," Kat said. "Look— I'm taking softball when Annie takes music. Besides, we're easy to tell apart once you get to know us, even without these necklaces. My face is wider and I have more freckles."

I peered at them and saw that Kat was right, but not by much. I had already figured out that Kat was the louder of the two, the one with all the ideas. She snorted when she laughed, smiled easily, and talked as if time was running out. Annie was quiet, but she was always tapping out a rhythm with her fingers. I thought of Annie as the drummer and Kat as the lead singer in a band. And Annie was neater than Kat, too. I'd noticed when they unpacked that Kat threw her stuff in her cubby in no particular order, but Annie placed her things in organized piles.

"I'd love to be a twin," Brooke said. "I'd play tricks on people all the time."

Kat grinned. "Well, ha! I'm not Kat! We switched necklaces this morning!"

What?

One twin gave the other a playful shove and said, "Stop it. She's kidding, you guys!"

Everyone laughed. Phew! Okay, so Kat was the jokester, too. Darby came in and told us we needed to get ready for bed. I was nervous about changing my clothes in front of all these new girls. Would people go to the bathroom to do it? Would they strip right in the middle of the cabin? I took my time selecting my pajamas and watched what the others did. Delaney started for the bathroom, but Kat and Annie just changed next to their bunk. I decided to be brave and follow their lead.

When Delaney came out, she unrolled a flat blue mat and said to us all, "I like to meditate before I go to sleep. I hope you don't mind."

I glanced at Tammy and raised my eyebrows. She smirked. But we all shrugged and said, "Sure," "No problem," and "Go right ahead."

Delaney sat cross-legged with her eyes closed and her hands cupped neatly in her lap. The rest of us went into the bathroom to brush our teeth. Brooke circled her finger next to her head as if to say Delaney was crazy. Tammy mouthed the word "Om." We all snickered. The water was running, so I was sure Delaney didn't hear. But still, I felt sort of bad for her. At the same time, I wished she wasn't my bunkmate.

It turned out I wasn't the only one who had brought a bedtime buddy to camp. Brooke had a newish-looking pink squish pillow in the shape of a heart. Delaney and Tammy had both brought their baby blankets. Delaney's was grayish yellow with a satin edge, and Tammy's was grayish white with holes in it. Kat and Annie hadn't brought anything, but that was probably because they had each other. I was glad I'd decided to bring Henry.

The mattress was so thin and lumpy, I didn't think I'd ever fall asleep. Plus, the crickets were too loud. And I heard everyone breathing. I rubbed Henry's nose and thought about home. At home, Mom and Dad would tuck me in, and Snowball would tap, tap, tap until I fell asleep. At home, I would change into my pajamas in private and I wouldn't have to flash my flat-as-a-pancake chest to five other developing girls. At home, I would go to sleep certain that Tammy was and would be my best friend forever.

I rolled over, and my glasses bumped the side of my nose. Oops. It seemed Mom was right. I took them off, but there was no place to put them. I didn't have a bedside table. On top of my cubby was Delaney's cubby. So I leaned over and tucked my glasses inside one of my shoes.

Tomorrow, I told myself. Tomorrow would be a better day.

• • •

I woke up Monday morning with a positive attitude. Here I was, at camp. The sun was shining. I remembered not to step on my glasses. And Tammy and I would be living together for the next four weeks.

We headed to breakfast in our pajamas. Darby assured us that that was the routine here at Star Lake. Joining a hundred campers in pj's made it feel like I was at a great big slumber party. I filled my plate with scrambled eggs, two sausage links, and a biscuit, and I poured a tall glass of red bug juice, which tasted like watered-down cherry Kool-Aid. Everyone seemed excited about our first full day at camp. We talked about our schedules, tried to decide if we should wear flip-flops or gym shoes, and if we should put our swimsuits on under our clothes or go back to the cabin to change before lake activities. Delaney was the only one who didn't participate in the conversation. She quietly ate her oatmeal with raisins, and I couldn't help thinking the raisins looked like little flies caught in a bowl of wet cement.

"Let's make a pact," Annie said. "Anyone who comes back to the cabin during morning activities has to keep the place clean."

"Here we go again," Kat said, shaking her head.

What was that about?

"I thought I left my mom in Chicago," Brooke said. "Who cares how clean the cabin is?"

"I do," Annie said.

"And you will, too," Kat explained. "The nurse inspects the cabins during morning activities and scores you from one to one hundred and you need an eighty to pass, and if you fail inspection you don't get canteen."

I had already found out that canteen was what they called the camp store. It was open each night, and you could buy candy, popcorn, Slushies, and pop. Oh, and boring things like stamps and batteries.

"And," Annie said, continuing for Kat, "the cabin with the highest score wins inspection. They're the 'Neat Guys,' and they get to work in canteen that night."

"Our cabin never won Neat Guys last year," Kat said with a guilty look on her face.

"She's a slob, in case you haven't noticed," Annie said.

"But I promise to do better this summer. I swear, no more wet towels and swimsuits on the cabin floor!"

Working in canteen sounded fun—pulling the lever to make a Slushie, scooping popcorn from a real popcorn maker—I'd love to do that.

"It's a pact," Tammy said, and we all put our hands together to seal it.

A bunch of older girls came by our table, and I recognized one as the girl from the parking lot with the long dark curls. She looked like she could be in a shampoo commercial, with her olive skin and shiny hair. She said, "Hey, Laney! How's it going?"

Delaney looked up from her oatmeal and smiled in a grateful sort of way. "Pretty good," she said quietly.

"Oh my gosh, Madison!" another girl said, elbowing the first. "Your sister is so cute with her bed head!"

That was Delaney's sister? They looked nothing alike. Delaney's hair was sticking up on one side of her head, and flat on the other. She tried to smooth it out, but it didn't work.

"Here," Madison said, and she took a ponytail holder off her wrist and handed it to Delaney, who gathered her hair into a lumpy ponytail. Madison had a whole row of elastic bands on one wrist, and a couple of friendship bracelets on the other. She was wearing a blue tank top and blue-and-gray flannel pajama pants. The rest of the girls she was with were all dressed just the same, but in different colors. I wondered if the counting-sheep pajama set I was wearing was too babyish for camp. If only the packing list had been more specific.

Madison introduced herself and her friends, and we all said hi. They were in Cabin One, the second oldest group of girls. Madison said, "I hope Laney hasn't been freaking you out with her meditating." She squeezed Delaney's shoulders in a friendly way. "She's the weird one of the family."

Everyone laughed—even Delaney. It was clear that Madison meant it in a joking way, but I could tell Delaney was uncomfortable. She licked her lips and looked down at her oatmeal. The thing was, a joke like that wasn't funny when it was true.

• • •

My morning activities zoomed by. In soccer, we played my favorite tag game, sharks and minnows, and I won. They evaluated us in tennis, and I was put in the intermediate group. In gymnastics, we worked on straddle rolls, cartwheels, and round-offs. The counselor said I pointed my toes very nicely.

By lunch I was starving, and I quickly discovered another reason to do well in inspection. Eddie called the tables up to eat according to how clean their cabins were. We scored a 93, which you would think was fantastic, but we were the third to last cabin to eat! Macaroni and cheese never looked so appetizing.

During rest hour the six of us decided to hang out on the grass in front of our cabin. Delaney brought her yoga mat outside and started stretching. The rest of us sprawled on towels. Kat and Annie listened to their iPods, and Tammy, Brooke, and I read *Archie* comic books and watched ants crawl through the grass. After a while I asked Tammy if she wanted to play War Madness.

"Oh my God!" she said. "We haven't played that in so long. Do you have cards?"

I nodded.

"What's War Madness?" Brooke asked.

"It's this game we made up when we were like what, eight?" Tammy asked.

"Maybe even younger."

"It's War, but when you win three hands in a row you get to make up a new rule or punishment for the other person. It gets kind of silly. But fun. Go get your cards, Jem."

I ran into the cabin and brought out a deck of cards. We played for the rest of the hour. By the end, Tammy was talking in an English accent and doing cartwheels before each turn, and I was speaking in pig Latin and flipping my cards over using only my toes. Not an easy feat! I was glad Brooke had kept her nose in her comic book and hadn't asked to join us. I'd never played War Madness with anyone besides Tammy, and I didn't think it would work with three people, anyway.

6

Finally it was time for sailing. Since Brooke was in this class with us, the partnering situation was going to be complicated. The only good thing was that Delaney was in our class, too. I hoped Delaney and Brooke would somehow partner up so I could be with Tammy.

At the boating dock, a counselor stood in front of a big whiteboard on wheels. "Hi, girls," she said. "I'm Nancy. And you are . . ." We introduced ourselves, and she checked us off on her clipboard. When Delaney said her last name, Nancy smiled widely. "You're Madison's little sister. How great! Girls, Delaney's sister is one of camp's best sailors. Last year she won the Star Lake Cup. So keep your eyes on Delaney here. I'm guessing she'll be a quick learner."

Delaney looked as if she wanted to hide behind one of the boulders along the shore of Star Lake.

"What's the Star Lake Cup?" I asked. It wasn't in the brochure.

"I'm glad you asked," Nancy said. "It's our big sailing race at the end of camp. Even though you girls are beginners, in four weeks you'll know everything you need to know to compete. The winners will get their names engraved on the Cup. Have you all seen it? It's on display in the Lodge. So, sailors, listen up, we have a lot to learn."

I couldn't wait to see the trophy. It sounded so cool. I imagined sailing to victory with Tammy. How perfect would that be?

Nancy wrote the word "WIND" on the white board. She looked at a girl in a blue bathing suit. "Zoey, can you tell me which direction the wind is coming from?"

Zoey pointed straight out toward Star Lake.

"Right," Nancy said. "And how do you know that?"

"I can feel it on my face?"

"Good," she said, writing "FEEL IT" on the board. "There are other ways to tell where the wind is coming from, too." Nancy explained about whitecaps and anchored boats pointing into the wind, and then she asked, "Delaney, why is it important to know where the wind is coming from?"

Delaney licked her lips and shrugged. She clearly did not have an answer. So much for following in her sister's footsteps.

47

"Are we going to sail today?" Brooke interrupted. "This feels like school."

What a dumb thing to say. When was the last time Brooke went to school in a bathing suit and flip-flops on the shore of a beautiful lake? I tried to catch Tammy's attention to see if she also thought Brooke was being ridiculous, but Tammy was twiddling a piece of grass between her fingers.

Nancy narrowed her eyes at Brooke for a moment. I was glad Brooke's rudeness didn't get past her. "Actually," Nancy said, "before you sail on your own, you'll have to pass a written test about safety rules and wind basics, and you'll have to rig a boat, and capsize and right it, so I hope you'll listen up." She looked around at all of us, waiting for anyone to challenge her.

Nobody did.

"Okay, then let's continue." She filled the board with diagrams of boats and sails and wind. She talked about tacking, reaching, coming about, and jibing. A lot of what she said went over my head, but I got the idea that you couldn't sail directly into the wind, because there wouldn't be any wind hitting the sail. Instead, you had to keep the wind at your side and sort of zigzag through the water. That was tacking. I wasn't sure what the difference was between coming about and jibing. They were both ways to turn, but for some reason, jibing was much more difficult and dangerous. I made a mental note never to jibe if I could help it, even though

I didn't have a clue what that meant. My head was spinning. I had no idea sailing would be so complicated. But that was okay. I was up for the challenge. Tammy and I would master this together.

Nancy said, "So, have I confused and scared you girls enough for one day?" We laughed nervously, and she said, "Not to worry. Before you know it, this will all be second nature. It's smart to be a little scared. These boats can go fast. If you don't follow the right-of-way and safety rules, you could injure yourself or someone else. Now follow me, and I'll show you how to rig a boat."

Nancy led the way into the boat shed. I blinked a few times as my eyes adjusted to the dim light. Along one wall were life jackets hung by size. Along the opposite wall were dinged-up wooden boat parts labeled centerboards and rudders and tillers. But taking up most of the shed were the sails, and the red, orange, and yellow sail I'd seen in the brochure was the first one I noticed. It was beautiful, like a sunset. The sails were attached to metal poles, the booms, which leaned diagonally against a beam near the roof along with the masts. Ropes, or sheets, as Nancy told us they were called, were coiled neatly and hung down from the booms. Each sail was a different combination of colors. I ran my fingers across the sunset sail and felt its smooth, strong texture.

"Okay, sailors," Nancy said. "Grab a partner, and carefully bring a sail out to a boat. Don't let the sail or the sheets drag on the ground."

I turned around to take Tammy's hand, but Brooke had beaten me to it. She wore a smug look on her face. Tammy pulled on her earlobe. "Sorry, Jem," she said.

My heart felt like it was going to explode. How had this happened again?

"Want to be my partner?" Delaney whispered, staring at her feet.

Of course I didn't. "I guess so," I said, and we waited our turn to pull a sail off the roof beam.

• • •

"There are three steps involved in getting your boat ready to sail," Nancy said into a bullhorn. We were all partnered off, standing waist-deep in Star Lake, ready to rig our boats. "First, slide the mast through the gooseneck on the lower boom and into the mast step hole."

"The what in the where?" I asked.

"Like this, I think," Delaney said, and she lifted the thickest of the three poles and slid it through a metal ring and into a snug hole on the boat's deck.

Not bad.

"Great, Delaney," Nancy said.

I saw a shy grin sneak out of the corners of Delaney's mouth. My toes squished into the sandy bottom of the lake as we waited for step number two. The other girls were taking a little longer getting their masts up.

"Step two: the rope that is threaded through the top

of the mast is called the halyard, girls. One of you will pull on the halyard, which raises the sail. The other one will lift the lower boom up to give an extra boost to the sail. You want the sail to be nice and high."

Brooke shouted, "We can't reach ours, Nancy!" The end of Brooke and Tammy's halyard was near the top of the mast, and Nancy had to stand on her tiptoes on their boat's deck to reach it. Ours was right where it was supposed to be.

"You wanna pull down?" I asked Delaney, and she nodded.

She tugged on the halyard, and the pink-and-white sail opened up. I lifted the boom to raise the sail even higher, and suddenly our boat looked like a real boat. Before Nancy could even tell us what to do next, Delaney led the tail of the halyard through a hole next to the mast, and wound it around a flat hook, holding it in place.

"How'd you know to do that?" I asked.

Delaney shrugged. "I don't know if I'm right, but it looks like that would make sense, doesn't it?"

I had to agree. And soon enough, Nancy told everyone to do exactly what Delaney had just done, but she called the hook a cleat. So maybe Delaney was going to take after her sister, after all. But still, she was strange. And quiet. And boring. I'd be having way more fun with Tammy. We'd be joking and laughing the whole time.

"Now for the last part of step two: the line that runs

along the lower boom is called the mainsheet," Nancy said. "This is the sheet you'll use to control the position of the sail. Hook the tail end of the mainsheet onto the traveler at the stern of the boat."

The stern was the back. I knew that much. And I guessed the traveler was that plastic-coated metal rope. So I hooked it up, and Delaney nodded. I peeked over at Tammy and Brooke. They were high-fiving each other.

For the third step in rigging the boat, we had to go back into the boat shed to bring out a centerboard and rudder. We snapped the rudder into place, being careful not to pinch our fingers in the springy thing, the pintle, a pin that held it together. We slid the centerboard into the slot in front of the cockpit, and we were ready to go.

But we didn't go anywhere.

Nancy had us take everything apart and put it all together again. Then she checked her watch and said, "Awesome job, girls! You all passed the first test. Put your sails away and head to your next class. Wednesday, you'll study for the written test and I'll give you some one-on-one training on the lake."

I couldn't wait.

• • •

At dinner, a bunch of girls were looking at the Star Lake Cup trophy. I had no idea how I'd missed it before. It was right there, over the fireplace. And it was huge. The top of the trophy was a big silver cup with handles on each side. It stood on three silver bases, each one smaller than the one below it. All over the bases were girls' names and nicknames. I found "Madison Reed and Lisa Cole: The Package." There were other nicknames: "Flying Friends," "Double Trouble," "Goofballs," and even "Gassers." I told Tammy we needed a nickname.

"What for?" Brooke asked, edging her way in between Tammy and me.

"For the trophy. Look. Everyone has one."

Brooke glanced at the trophy, then shrugged. "It only matters if you win. And besides, Tammy and I are sailing partners. We're the ones who need a nickname."

All of a sudden, my heart felt ten times too big for my chest. Sure, they'd been partners today, but that didn't mean they'd be partners every day. Did it? I couldn't be stuck with Delaney for the next month. "You think you're permanent partners just because you happened to be standing next to Tammy in the boat shed?" I put my hands on my hips. "That's not how it works, Brooke."

Brooke blinked, and her eyes filled with tears. I squinted at her. Was she for real?

Tammy put her arms around both of us. "You guys, this is dumb. Who cares? We don't have to pick partners now, anyway."

Brooke sniffled and blinked, keeping her tears from

spilling out of her eyes. My nose tingled, and I thought I might cry. But that was stupid. I was not the crying type. It was just that I felt so loose and wobbly, like I didn't know where I belonged. Because of Brooke. It was all because of Brooke.

• • •

That night I got a popcorn and Slushie at canteen. Then we had a sing-along at the lakeshore. The night sky here was so different from the one at home. The moon was brighter. Clearer. And a gazillion stars twinkled in the black sky. Was it just two nights ago that I had wished on the star that was really an airplane? If I'd known then that Brooke was coming to camp, I would have found a real star and rewished.

At bedtime, Kat and Annie gave each other back rubs. So did Tammy and Brooke. Delaney offered to give me one, but I said no thanks, even though I wouldn't have minded a massage. My whole body ached from running around at my activities all day. I squeezed Henry tight, rubbed his nose, and thought of something positive to help me fall asleep. The image that came to mind was sailing. In the sunset boat with Tammy. Racing to victory in the Star Lake Cup. Somehow or other, I needed to make that happen.

7

On Tuesday, Brooke skied around the lake on her very first try. I did everything Darby and Todd Casey, the boat driver, said to do, but I never even got to standing. As soon as the boat took off, I fell forward out of my tucked position, and the towrope flew out of my hands. After four attempts, Darby said it was the next person's turn. What a bust!

At least I moved away from the dock with each try, so I was far enough from shore to need a lift back to camp in the boat. I took off the huge, awkward skis and swam over to the side of the boat. I handed the skis to Darby. Then she pulled me up by my life jacket, and I tumbled into the boat. I was out of breath and cold, and my bathing suit was stuck in my butt. But I was in the boat with Todd Casey, and even without my glasses, I could tell he was the cutest guy I'd ever seen. He winked at me, smiled a crooked smile, and said, "Good try, Jemma." Oh my gosh, he knew my name! He wasn't wearing a shirt, and his skin was smooth and tan and perfect. His shoulder-length shaggy brown hair was windblown, and I knew I was staring at him for too long, but I couldn't help myself.

Darby said, "Jemma," and she wiped at her nose in a real exaggerated way. Oh, embarrassment! She was telling me to wipe my own nose. I felt my cheeks flush. I would have liked to jump overboard right that instant! But Darby laughed, and so did I. It figured the first time I was ever that close to a gorgeous, hunky guy, I'd have a booger hanging out of my nose. Not that it really mattered. Todd was probably ten years older than I was. But lucky Darby. She got to sit in the boat with him all day long, and she was just the right age for him, too.

• • •

After skiing, Brooke and I were in the cabin, changing out of our swimsuits. It was the first time we'd been alone together, and I had no idea what to say to her. I stared into my cubby, as if choosing the right pair of shorts and T-shirt was the most important thing in the world. Brooke was ignoring me, too. The silence between us seemed stupid, somehow, so I decided to be friendly. "Great job at skiing." I stepped into underpants and navy blue shorts, keeping my towel strategically wrapped around me. "You made it look so easy."

With her back to me, Brooke pulled on a sports bra and a red shirt. "It is easy."

Was that an insult? I wasn't sure, but she saw me struggle today. "For you, maybe. You probably ski all the time in California, right?" I had to drop my towel then, to get my shirt on, so I turned away from Brooke.

"I live in Sacramento, not on the ocean." She paused, then said quietly, "Lived, I mean."

I heard the regret in her voice, and to my surprise I felt sorry for her.

"I've never skied before today," Brooke continued.

Fully dressed, I faced her. "Oh, I just thought because you said you know how to surf—"

"I learned that on vacation." She turned around and stared at me as if I was a big doofus. "I guess some people are just more coordinated than others." She tightened her ponytail and strutted out of the cabin. The screen door banged shut.

I stood blinking, my breath caught in my throat. So much for being friendly to Brooke.

The bell rang for second period—ranching with Tammy. Thank goodness!

• • •

I headed over to the camp's farm, which was located behind the gym, and I saw Tammy right away.

"Hey, how was skiing?" she asked.

"Harder than you'd think. I never got up. But I did get to ride in the boat with Todd Casey."

"No, I mean, how did you and Brooke get along?"

"Oh. That wasn't so easy, either." I was about to tell her about Brooke's rude comment when Mallory, the ranching counselor, asked us all to quiet down so we could get started.

Mallory gave us a tour of the farm: a small red barn with pigs and a Shetland pony named Wayne, a vegetable garden, a duck pond, and a pen that held rabbits and goats. After she explained the safety rules to us, we got to play with the animals, or, as Mallory said, "begin to develop a trusting relationship with them."

Tammy and I unlatched the door to the rabbit hutch and each carefully lifted out a bunny. Mine was white with red eyes, and Tammy's was the color of caramel. We sat in the grass with the bunnies in our laps, and Tammy asked, "So what did you mean before, about Brooke?"

I ran my fingers through the bunny's fur and felt its small body tremble. "She called me uncoordinated."

Tammy laughed. "Really?"

"It's not funny." Was I missing something here?

Tammy smoothed her bunny's long ears. "You know you're coordinated, Jemma. You're one of the most athletic people I know. I'm sure she was kidding."

It didn't seem like she was kidding.

"Brooke's got a weird sense of humor. But she's terrific once you get to know her."

My bunny nuzzled its nose into the crook of my elbow. I didn't like the way this conversation was going. It was as if Tammy was telling me I had to like Brooke. As if she and Brooke were a package deal. "Why do you care so much about me and her getting along?" I asked.

"Well, I told you, she's going through a hard time. I want her to have a fantastic summer. I want us all to be friends."

"I don't see how that's going to happen."

"What are you talking about?" Tammy sounded annoyed.

"Never mind. What was up with that letter? The one Brooke didn't open."

Tammy looked around to make sure nobody was listening. "It was from her dad."

"And?"

"Well, she's pretty mad at him right now."

"How come?"

Tammy didn't say anything for a second. She scratched her bunny between his ears. Then she said, "I kind of feel bad talking about this with you, Jem. No offense, or anything. It's just private stuff, and I don't think Brooke would like me talking about it. With anyone. You know?"

So Tammy and Brooke had secrets. I pushed away that punched-in-the-heart feeling. It's okay, I told myself. "Well, can I ask you something else?" Tammy nodded. "What was the deal Brooke was talking about? You know, with you guys bunking together?"

"Oh, that." Tammy waved her hand as if it was nothing. As if we hadn't planned on bunking together in the first place. "Brooke didn't want to come to camp. And her mom sort of made her. And part of the deal was that I would bunk with her."

"Part of the deal?"

"Yeah. And I said I'd hang with her. You know, make sure she's okay. Making friends. Having fun. Stuff like that."

"So you're doing this because of a deal?"

Tammy rolled her eyes. "No, Jemma. Oh my God. She's my cousin. And my friend. And she's really cool. You just have to give her a chance. Why are you acting like this? Why can't you be friends with her?"

"I don't know," I said. "But . . . it's not as if she wants to be friends with me, either."

"Oh, Jemma, of course she does." Tammy smiled gently, and I wanted to believe her. I wanted it to be true. Then maybe I wouldn't feel so crowded out. But I was pretty sure Tammy was wrong.

I shrugged. "You know, I didn't realize she'd be here until she showed up. I mean, when we first planned to go to camp together, it was just the two of us. It was your idea. Remember?"

There was an awkward minute where neither of us

said anything. I was remembering the phone conversation we'd had over winter break. Tammy had called me all excited about finding this camp. She'd said it would be the perfect reunion for us. She'd told me to beg my parents if I had to, do the dishes for a year, clean out the garage, anything to convince them. And the funny thing was, I didn't have to beg my parents. They signed me up right away.

I wondered if Tammy was thinking of that same phone conversation. Or had she forgotten it, the way she'd forgotten that we'd planned to bunk together? Tammy was petting her bunny, avoiding my eyes. I didn't like the idea of having to be friends with Brooke. But fighting with Tammy was the worst. If I fought with her, I'd lose her to Brooke. Then I'd be all alone. It was better to pretend everything was fine. So I held my bunny up, moved his front paw back and forth, and started humming the tune to "The Bunny Hop."

Tammy laughed, relieved, and we both stood up and danced.

Dear Mom, Dad, and Derek,

Camp is different than I expected. There's a big sailing race at the end of the summer. The trophy is awesome, and I think that maybe Tammy and I are going to try to win it. The girls in my cabin are so-so. There are these twins I like, but there's another girl who is very quiet and really into yoga.

which is kind of weird, don't you think? And Brooke is not the nicest. But I am trying to give her a chance.

Gotta go. Kat (one of the twins) is going to teach me a card game called Spit. I don't think it involves any actual spitting.

Love you! W.B.S. (write back soon) xoxoxoxoxo to infinity . . .

Jemma

During rest hour, Delaney practiced yoga while the rest of us had a Spit tournament and listened to Annie play the bongos she'd brought from home. Spit was a fast game with a lot of card slapping involved, and Annie was beating out all kinds of rhythms on her drums, but Delaney acted as if she didn't even hear us. She just pretzeled herself into different positions, her face focused in concentration. Why did she come to camp in the first place? It seemed she'd have been just as happy stuck on a desert island with her yoga mat.

8

At our next sailing class, Nancy passed out a three-page handout to each of us as soon as we arrived, and told us we'd take a test at the end of the period. She also had us pick numbers from a hat to determine in which order we'd go sailing with her. I was fourth. While I waited my turn, I sat in the grass with the other girls and studied.

There sure was a lot to learn. We'd need to know all the parts of the boat, the different points of sail, the right-of-way rules, and a bunch of nautical terms. I liked to make connections in my head to help me remember new things. So I thought about how "port" had four letters, just like the word "left," and port was the left side of the boat. And "bow" was the front of the boat, and when you bow, you face forward. I read the definitions of "coming about" and "jibing," but I still didn't understand why jibing was so dangerous. Coming about was turning when you were sailing toward the wind, and jibing was turning when you were sailing away from the wind. It seemed to me that they were kind of the same thing.

Finally it was my turn to sail with Nancy, so I put on a life jacket and waded out to the boat. It was the one with the pink-and-green sail. In my head, I called it the preppy boat. Nancy smiled and said, "Welcome aboard, mate."

I hopped onto the boat and swung my feet into the cockpit, and right away a gust of wind powered us over the lake.

"We're going to use our sailing terms here," Nancy said, handing me the mainsheet. "I'm the skipper because I'm steering the boat with this . . . Do you know what it's called?"

"The tiller?"

"Right. Whichever direction I push the tiller, the boat will turn the opposite way. So if I push it port, the boat will turn . . ."

"Starboard?"

"Right again. And you are the first mate because you are in charge of the sail. Watch what happens when you let the sail out."

I let the mainsheet slide a bit through my fingertips, and the sail began to flutter.

"That's called luffing. Now start pulling the sail in, and stop as soon as it becomes taut again."

I did what she said, and Nancy exclaimed, "Perfect! That's exactly where you want the sail to be. You're a natural!"

I couldn't help but smile. I loved the feel of the wind in my hair and the boat slapping against the lake, splashing water up at me. My glasses got a little misty, but I didn't even care.

Nancy showed me the difference between beating—sailing toward the wind—and reaching—sailing with the wind basically coming from the side. She quizzed me on the boat parts and a few other things. Then, much sooner than I'd have liked, she turned the boat around and headed back to shore.

"Any questions?" she asked.

I had a ton. I wanted to ask about jibing, but the more important one had to do with partners. "I was wondering, with the partners we had last time, are those permanent assignments?"

"They don't have to be. But if you want, that's fine with me," Nancy said. "You and Delaney worked really well together."

"Yeah, thanks." I smiled, relieved. I had the answer I wanted. There was no reason to tell Nancy that despite how well Delaney and I worked together, I wasn't interested in being her partner again. It was going to be Tammy and me from here on out.

···

At dinner, Brooke got another one of those letters from her dad that she didn't open. Tammy got one from her parents and three from friends at school, including one from Lindsey, which was actually written to both Brooke and Tammy. I got one from Derek.

Dear Jemma,

Mom took me to the zoo today. And guess what? I saw an elephant peeing. It was like a bathtub faucet. I've never seen so much pee in my life. You would have cracked up.

From, Your Amazing Brother Derek

I laughed and said, "You guys gotta hear this." Then I read it to my cabin.

Everyone started to laugh, but Brooke said, "That's disgusting. Nobody wants to hear about elephant pee when we're about to eat."

The laughter died quickly, and Tammy said, "It is kind of bad timing, Jem." She held up a pitcher of lemonade to prove her point.

I wasn't so sure. I bet Brooke just didn't want me to be the center of attention. And why was Tammy taking her side again? I thought about saying, "Pass the elephant pee, please." But I didn't. Chances were, nobody would get the joke.

• • •

For that night's evening program, each cabin had to make up a song and dance to introduce themselves to the camp. So after dinner we headed back to the cabin to work on our presentation. We had about an hour to do it.

"This place is a mess," Annie said. She was right. There were towels, clothes, stationery, and markers strewn all over the floor. "We need space to work. Let's do a thirty-second pickup now, and tomorrow morning we'll barely have to clean at all. Maybe we'll even be the Neat Guys!"

Brooke plopped onto her bunk. "I don't feel like cleaning." She held her unopened letter up to the light. Then she tossed it into her cubby before rolling over and facing the wall. Tammy sat on the edge of Brooke's bed and patted her back.

Kat asked, "Are you homesick?"

Brooke sniffled and nodded her head.

"Well, we can clean up without you. Right, guys?"

Everyone but me shrugged in approval. Was I the only one who thought that was unfair? Homesick or not, she shouldn't be so lazy. Besides, Eddie told the whole camp the best cure for homesickness was to keep busy. Lying on your bunk, imagining what might be inside an unopened letter from your dad, would only make things worse. But I wasn't about to say that out loud and suffer another dirty look from Brooke.

"Okay, then," Annie said. "We did this all the time last summer. Quick and painless, like ripping off a Band-Aid. On your mark, get set, go!"

We all counted back from thirty and ran around the cabin, tossing clothes in laundry bags, shoving shoes under beds, hanging up wet towels, and putting stationery and cards away in our cubbies. We finished with five seconds to spare. "Awesome!" Kat said. "Now, who has ideas for songs?"

Brooke turned over and stared at us with wet eyes.

"What about 'Take Me Out to the Ball Game'?" I suggested. It was one of the few songs I could sing in tune.

"That's a good one," Kat said.

But Brooke said, "No. That's boring. What about some kind of show tune? Like from *Grease*?"

I guessed Brooke was feeling better. At least she wasn't too homesick to put my ideas down.

"Yeah," Tammy said. "How about 'Summer Nights'? I love that song!" She sang a line from the song into an imaginary microphone.

"Great idea," Kat said. "Who wants to be the secretary?"

"I will," Delaney said quietly. She got out paper and a marker so she could write down lyrics as we made them up.

"We want everyone at camp to remember who we

are," Annie explained. "So we have to include some interesting information in the song."

"And we have to have some cool dance moves," Kat added, kicking and twirling.

"What if we can't dance?" I asked.

"No worries," Kat said. "I'll choreograph some simple steps for you and you can be in the background. Who else can't dance?"

"Tammy can't," I said.

"Yes, I can!"

"Since when?"

"At school this year we had dances, and I did fine."

"You mean like boy-girl dances? In fifth grade?" I asked. Tammy nodded. Wow. They sure did things faster in the city.

"We had dances, too," Brooke said. "Didn't you?"

"No." The way she asked made me feel embarrassed, which was stupid because a minute ago I didn't care that I'd never been to a school dance before. "But we'll have them next year in middle school. Besides, the boys in fifth grade at our school wouldn't dance with girls, anyway. They didn't even talk to us."

"That's hilarious," Brooke said. "I've already had two boyfriends."

"Real boyfriends?" I asked, not believing her.

"Yep."

"Did you kiss them?" Kat asked.

"One of them."

"Cool!" Kat and Annie said at the same time.

Kat, Annie, and Tammy listened attentively while Brooke told all about this boy Joseph who kissed her at one of their dances. Big whoop. As if that made her the queen of cool. Personally, I thought fifth grade was much too young for kissing. I noticed that Delaney didn't seem interested in Brooke's story, either. She was sitting on the floor, doodling on the edges of her paper. I sat next to her and waited for a pause in the conversation.

Then I said, "The song, you guys. Remember? We have to make up a song."

Kat looked at her watch and yelped. "Yikes! We only have half an hour. Come on, let's focus."

After a while we had the song together, and I had to admit, it was pretty good.

The part about me went:

Tell me more, tell me more, Jemma's next in
    line.
Tell me more, tell me more, don't you think
    we're divine?
Uh-huh, uh-huh, uh-huh do do do do.
Jemma's sporty, she loves to play ball,
Soccer, tennis, and that's not all,
She tries hard, she loves to compete,
She's a girl that you'll all want to meet!

Oh whoa! Summer days, drifting away, but oh!
　　Cabin Six is the best.
Wella wella, wella uh!

Annie drummed on her bongos for part of it, which sounded really cool. And the dancing wasn't too hard. Maybe I could dance, after all.

9

Thanks to our super fast cleanup the night before, our cabin was spotless the next day, and I was sure we were going to be the Neat Guys. But at lunch Eddie announced that Cabin Three had won for the third day in a row, and we all groaned.

"Last year this happened, too," Annie complained. "It was Cabin Eight, though. They won almost every day. I think it must be the cubbies. I bet they look inside our cubbies and take points off for crumpled clothes!"

We'd never win inspection if that was true.

"No way," Brooke said. "That's an invasion of privacy."

"Last year Eddie threw a cell phone in the lake," Kat said. "It belonged to a girl from Woods, and everyone said they found it during inspection, so you never know, they might look in our cubbies."

"He threw it in the lake?" Tammy asked.

"He really doesn't like cell phones," Kat said.

While everyone was talking about the cell-phone-in-the-lake rumor, I placed my finger on my nose. We played this game called Noses at every meal. One of us put her finger on her nose, and as soon as another noticed, she put her finger on her nose, too. The last person to do it had to wipe the table at the end of the meal.

Brooke was the last to notice. But she shook her head and said, "It doesn't count because we haven't gotten our food yet."

I said, "Nobody ever made a rule like that."

And she said, "Well, I'm officially making it a rule."

And I said, "Fine."

And she said, "Fine."

And then we glared at each other.

Then Tammy said, "Come on, Jemma!" as if this was all my fault. How unfair! Everyone knew if you made up a rule after you lost a game, you couldn't expect the rule to be retroactive. But I didn't say anything. I wasn't sure why. Maybe because I was so shocked by Tammy's response, not just to Noses but to everything this summer. I was beginning to wonder if I even knew her anymore.

I noticed Delaney looking at me sympathetically. At

least she was on my side. But she wasn't exactly going to help my cause. Aligning with the cabin weirdo was not a smart move. I bet that's exactly what Brooke wanted, for me to become friends with Delaney so she could have Tammy all to herself. Well, it was not going to happen. No way!

"Cabin Six," Eddie said into the microphone. "You scored a ninety-eight. Help yourselves to lunch, ladies."

Our best score yet. At least something was going in the right direction. I pushed my chair back and got in line.

• • •

Friday afternoon, Delaney, Tammy, Brooke, and I were walking down the hill to sailing class when I decided to ask Tammy if we could be partners before Brooke had a chance to beat me to it. Tammy took a quick peek at Brooke, then said, "Sure. Hey, Brooke, you want to sail with Delaney today?"

Brooke's shoulders sagged. "I guess."

Delaney didn't say anything. She just kept walking, staring straight ahead, as if it didn't bother her that she was clearly everyone's last choice. I didn't know how she did it. I felt sort of sorry for her again, but I was so excited to sail with Tammy that I didn't have time to dwell on it.

We'd all passed our written test, and now we had to capsize. Tammy and I rigged the red, orange, and yellow sunset boat, and after one mishap with the mast ending up on the wrong side of the boom, we got it right. Delaney was rigging the pink-and-white cotton-candy boat, and Brooke stood next to her, pointing here and there but not actually doing anything. Today Delaney's shirt said SHE WHO SMILES FIRST WINS. I thought it was dorky when I first saw it, but I decided to test it out. I smiled at Brooke. She rolled her eyes at me and turned away. Did that mean I'd won?

I hoped Tammy saw me smiling at Brooke. And I hoped she realized that Delaney was doing all the work while Brooke was acting bratty just because she didn't get the partner she wanted.

Nancy checked our boat and said, "Great job, girls. Now, don't go any farther than that buoy over there, and I'll watch you capsize."

I took a seat in the boat and held on to the mainsheet and the tiller. Tammy unhooked the boat from the buoy and hopped on board. "Do you want to be the skipper or first mate?" I asked.

"I'll be the skipper."

"Okay." I scooted over so Tammy could hold the tiller, and I grasped the mainsheet. The sail flapped back and forth uselessly, and the boat rocked in the small waves. "I think we're stuck," I said.

"We're in irons," Tammy said. "We're pointing straight into the wind. What did Nancy say about that again?"

"You need to push the tiller all to one side."

Tammy tried one direction, then the other. Nothing happened other than that our boat started moving backward toward the shore.

Nancy's voice rang through her bullhorn. "Jemma, push the boom out to catch the wind! And, Tammy, keep the tiller where you have it!"

We did as she said, and all of a sudden I felt the sail catch the wind, and we were on our way. Yes! The sail was bright and beautiful against the clear blue sky. I was amazed that we were skimming across the water, powered only by wind. It felt like magic.

As we got closer to the buoy, Tammy said, "Wait! What are we supposed to do again?"

"You push the tiller that way, and I pull the sail in, and I think we'll just tip over. Right?"

"Right. That's what Nancy said. And watch out for the boom. We don't want any head injuries today," Tammy said, imitating Nancy.

"Okay," I said. "But tomorrow is a different story. Tomorrow, head injuries are welcome at Camp Star Lake."

Tammy laughed. "Here we go!" She pushed the tiller and squealed.

Ahhhh! All of a sudden I felt the boat go up, up, up; then I slid right into Star Lake. I went under for a second, but I popped right back up, laughing. I was wading in the water near Tammy. The boat was on its side, the sail sprawled next to us. "That was awesome!"

"I know!" she said. "But we have to get the boat up before it turtles."

Nancy had warned us about that. If the boat tipped all the way upside down, the centerboard could slip out and float away. Then it would be really hard to get the boat right side up, and just about impossible to sail. So we swam around to the other side of the boat and pushed down on the end of the centerboard. The boat rose, with its sail dripping. So simple!

Nancy yelled from the shore, "Jemma and Tammy, great job! You're free to sail. But stay within eyesight!"

We climbed back into the boat and got situated. My glasses had water spots all over them, and I had no way to clean them out on the lake. I wished they came with miniature windshield wipers.

"Where to?" Tammy asked.

"Anywhere you want."

Tammy pointed us away from camp, and we were off. I let the sail out until it started to luff, then I pulled it in a tiny bit, the way Nancy had taught me. The bow of our boat slapped against the water, and sprays of mist splashed us as we sailed. I was so happy to be in the sunset boat with Tammy. It was my dream.

Tammy turned around and shaded her eyes with her hand. "Look. Brooke and Delaney just capsized."

I watched them tip the cotton-candy boat back up. Tammy cheered for them before turning back to me.

Okay, so maybe this wasn't exactly as I'd dreamed it would be. But at least Brooke was in a different boat, and we were sailing away from her.

We glided across Star Lake, not saying much to each other. I knew sometimes it was fine not to talk. Tammy and I had had plenty of times when being quiet together felt perfect. But this didn't feel like one of those. It felt more like there was so much that we weren't saying. That we couldn't say. Like that I wished Brooke wasn't at camp. And that I was afraid Tammy didn't like me half as much as she used to. I knew I wouldn't say any of that aloud. Because here we were, just the two of us in the sunset sailboat, and I wasn't going to ruin the moment.

So I said, "Remember the time we wrote that love song for Mr. Bradley?"

"Yes! Tracy was so mad at us!"

"Not half as mad as your parents were the time we spilled Orange Crush all over the new sofa!"

"I know. We thought they wouldn't notice if we turned the cushion over, but that didn't exactly work."

I laughed. "Yeah, I can still remember your mom's reaction when she saw the stain. 'God bless America, Tamera! How many times have I told you not to eat in the living room!' "

"You know I'm in trouble when she calls me Ta-mera."

"Or when she says, 'God bless America!' She's the only person I know who can make that sound like a curse."

"That *is* a curse for my mom!"

I laughed, and we continued rehashing old stories: the time Tammy rescued a baby robin that had fallen out of its nest; the time we had a lemonade sale and donated our whopping $4.81 to the local animal shelter.

"Remember how we used to think we would marry twin brothers and live next door to each other?" Tammy asked.

Used to think? "It could happen," I said.

Tammy laughed. "Oh, Jemma, please. That's so second grade."

My stomach tightened. "Yeah, I know." In that moment, I did know, and I was embarrassed for thinking such immature thoughts. I looked up at the sail and made a small adjustment. "We should probably start heading back," I said. "Do you know how to turn this boat around?"

She shook her head. "Do you?"

I laughed. "We're in trouble now! I don't want to jibe, and I'm not sure what that even means. We have to do the easier turn. We have to come about."

"Okay. So how do we do that?"

"Let's see. The sail is on our right, the starboard

side. So the wind is on our left. Port. So we have to turn left, which means we have to push the tiller right. Right?"

Tammy shrugged. "If you say so."

"Well, it's either that or we capsize the boat and point it toward camp before we tip it back up. That's always an option."

Tammy said, "No, we can do this. Let's give it a try."

So she pushed the tiller toward the sail, and I pulled the mainsheet in. And, whoosh, the boat started to turn. We ducked as the boom swung over our heads. Then we scooted to the other side, distributing the weight more evenly. "We did it!" Tammy said, and we gave each other high fives.

Camp looked so pretty from way out here in the middle of the lake. Even through my spotty glasses, I made out the skiing dock, the swimming dock, and the boating dock. And there was the riding ring, and the soccer field and the Lodge at the top of the hill. Part of me wanted to stay out here in this little boat with Tammy forever. "This is the best moment I've had at camp so far," I told her.

"It is peaceful."

"And we're pretty good sailors. Look how well we did today."

"Uh-huh."

We sailed quietly for a bit, and the silence felt better than before. I was just enjoying the lake with Tammy.

Finally I said, "I know the Star Lake Cup is a long time from now, but can't you see us winning?"

"I don't know about that, Jem!"

"Why not?"

"We're just beginners, for one thing."

"Yeah, but Nancy said we'd know everything we need to compete."

"True."

"And you know my motto. If you're going to do something, you might as well be good at it!"

"So you're going to be the best sailor at camp?"

"No. *We're* going to be the best sailors at camp."

Tammy laughed.

"I'm serious!"

"Okay, okay! We'll be the best sailors at Camp Star Lake. We'll win the Star Lake Cup. And we'll get our names engraved on that trophy. Is that the plan?"

"Yes, that's the plan!" I felt a smile spread across my face, and I started to think about a nickname that could go on the Cup. Maybe BFF. Or Friends to the End. Something like that. Brooke would have to find her own partner for the race.

10

That night it rained so hard the evening program was canceled. We were supposed to have gone into town to see the Lake Gliders Water-Ski Show, but instead we played Bingo in the Lodge. Eddie dressed up as Elvis in a white leisure suit and a funny wig, and in between games, he played Elvis music and we all got up and danced. We used M&M's as our Bingo markers, and the counselors kept refilling our bowls as we ate them. I was having fun, even though Brooke kept giving me her "look." Ever since sailing that afternoon, she'd been grouchy, and I'd done my best to stay out of her way. Meanwhile, the rain came down in sheets, and Star Lake was transformed into a dark, raging river.

Right in the middle of a Fill-your-whole-card round of Bingo, the lights in the Lodge flickered off, then on, then off again. Everyone screamed. It was so loud that I was terrified until I caught Tammy's eyes. We both had our mouths open wide, mid-scream, but suddenly it seemed hilarious, and we started to laugh.

The lights came back on, and Eddie spoke into his microphone in a calm voice. "Okay, girls, it's okay. Let's all move away from the windows. All the cabins over there, I want you to carefully pick up your Bingo cards and join the girls at the center tables. Make room, now. That's right." Eddie's instructions scared me again. We had to move away from the windows? What in the world did he think could happen?

I flinched when lightning struck close enough that I saw the zigzag line hit the lake. I reached for my Bingo board, and at that exact moment Brooke put her hand on it and slid all my M&M's onto the table.

"Hey!" I said. "I only needed four more!"

Brooke looked at me as if that couldn't be her problem. "And?"

"And you just knocked all my pieces off!"

"I did?" Brooke pretended not to realize what she had obviously done on purpose. "Oh, I'm sorry." She put her hand to her cheek in mock surprise.

That Brooke Bernstein! How in the world did Tammy like her? I narrowed my eyes at her and flung her card up. Her M&M's bounced to the floor.

Tammy said, "Jemma! What are you doing?"

"Brooke messed up my card."

"Accidentally," Brooke said.

Oh, please. You have got to be kidding me, I thought. Kat, Annie, Delaney, and some other girls who were standing nearby stared at us. Tammy looked at me questioningly, as if I needed to explain my bad behavior. "It's Brooke's fault," I blurted. "She started it!" Hadn't anyone seen?

"Are you kidding?" Brooke acted as though I was completely making this up.

Delaney licked her lips, then said, "You did, Brooke. I saw."

Everyone looked at Delaney. Brooke sneered at her.

Tammy said, "I'm sure it was an accident. Why would Brooke purposely knock your M&M's to the ground?"

I thought of three reasons off the top of my head. One, she couldn't stand letting me win anything, not even a dumb game of Bingo. Two, she was jealous that I'd sailed with Tammy today. And three, she was an evil human being who took pleasure in making other people suffer. But all these girls were staring at me as if I was the bad guy. All but Delaney, that is.

Darby came up and put her arm around me. "What's going on?" she asked.

"Nothing," I said, glowering at Brooke. "We just accidentally bumped into each other's cards."

"Oh, that's too bad," Darby said. "But there'll be more games."

I nodded. Of course there would be more games. And more activities. And more competition. And every step of the way, I would need to deal with Brooke. Tammy was convinced Brooke was funny and innocent. She didn't see the real picture. I remembered when I flunked the school vision test in third grade. I thought I'd been seeing just fine, and I was sure the school nurse had made a terrible mistake. But when I finally got glasses, I realized what I'd been missing. I was shocked that trees didn't look like big green blobs, that they had thousands of individual leaves, that brick walls had specks of different color and texture, and that some people's eyes sparkled, even from far away. If only I could fit Tammy with a pair of glasses that would show her the real Brooke. But maybe that was impossible. Maybe I wasn't even seeing the real Tammy anymore.

I stared out the window as Eddie called the numbers to finish the game. Lightning danced in the sky, and the anchored sailboats tossed and bobbed in the waves. The wind blew so hard that the trees bent over until they practically touched the ground. Then, all of a sudden, a canoe flew up the hill!

I screamed and put my hands over my head, thinking that the canoe would come smashing through the windows. Everyone turned to look. The canoe bounced end over end, out of control, and finally came to rest on the basketball court. How weird—a canoe blown about like a scrap of paper. The wind had done that.

The same wind that had gently powered our sunset sail-boat today.

• • •

Later at bedtime, after we had dashed to our cabins during a lull in the storm, the thunder and rain made our cabin seem cozy and safe. When I thought most everyone was asleep, I climbed out of bed and peeked into Delaney's. Her back was to me, and I wasn't sure if she was still awake. "Thanks," I whispered. "For tonight."

Delaney rolled over and smiled.

• • •

At waterskiing on Saturday, Brooke crossed the wake, the big V-shaped wave that motorboats leave behind them. She went over and back, over and back—on her first try.

Everyone clapped and cheered when she gracefully skied back to shore. I acted just as happy for her as the others did. After all, that's what a Firelighter would do. A Firelighter wouldn't hold a grudge. I plastered a smile to my face and pushed away all my negative thoughts. As Todd pulled the boat up for the next person, I heard Darby say, "Brooke, amazing job! I've never seen anyone take to skis so quickly before. Way to go, hon!"

"Yeah," I said. "Way to go."

I let everyone ski before me. On Thursday, time had

run out before I could take my turn. But today I wasn't so lucky.

"You're up, Jemma," Darby said.

I slid off the dock and into the lake. I was glad most of the kids, including Brooke, had already gone back to their cabins to change. At least I didn't have an audience.

"Now remember," Darby said, "let the boat pull you up. Don't let go of the tow bar. Back straight. Arms straight. Knees bent. Okay?"

"Got it." The thing was, I did get it. My mind got it completely. But for some reason, my body just wouldn't listen.

"And you might want to take off your glasses," Todd added.

I reached up and realized I did have my glasses on. "Oops! Thanks," I said. It wasn't easy to maneuver with the skis on, and just getting my glasses over to the dock took me a while. Then I had to move back out again, catch the towrope, and get situated. The tips of my skis dipped into the water, and I flailed around trying to get into the ready position. At last I was tucked in a ball, holding the towrope between my skis. "Hit it!" I shouted.

Todd revved the engine, pulled forward, and immediately the tow bar flew out of my hand. Oh, why couldn't I hold on to that stupid rope?

We repeated the ugly process four more times before I got into the boat with Todd and Darby. "You'll get it, Jemma," Todd said, and he smiled that crooked smile at me again.

My heart sped up. I had to admit, even though I knew he was about a million years too old, I couldn't help reacting. Darby was sitting in the seat next to Todd, sort of leaning in toward him. Why hadn't they fallen in love? Maybe I could help. When Todd pulled up to the dock, I told Darby she was burning on the back of her shoulders.

"Am I?" she said, touching her skin. Todd grabbed a bottle of sunscreen and offered to rub it in for her.

Look at me, a matchmaker!

11

Saturday night we had a social with Camp Thunder Ridge, a boys' camp. Getting ready for it could have been its own evening program. First there was a huge line at the shower house with a hundred girls wanting to shower at the same time. Then there was the drama of choosing outfits. Everyone in our cabin (not counting Delaney) traded clothes until we were happy with our look, and until we got final approval from Kat and Annie. Being experienced campers, they were quick to point out what was cool: flip-flops, low-rise jeans, and tight tops to show off our curves. Yes, four out of the six of us had curves. Brooke's chest was so developed, it was almost disturbing. Kat, Annie, and Tammy were all just starting. It didn't seem to matter to the others that I didn't have any curves, and I ended up wearing a clingy purple tie-dyed shirt of Annie's and my denim miniskirt. I drew the line at makeup, though. I mean, we were at camp. In the wilderness. What was the point of makeup? But the other girls in my cabin (not counting Delaney) put on lip gloss, eyeliner, and mascara.

Now we stood outside the buses and spritzed each other with bug spray. "Where's Delaney?" Kat asked.

I hadn't seen her since she threw on a pair of jeans and one of her yoga tops about an hour ago.

Tammy said, "I saw her walk off toward the ranch before."

"Ew," Brooke said. "She's going to smell like farm animals. Why would she go to the ranch before a social?" Everyone shrugged. Then Brooke swung her arms like a Broadway-bound farmer and sang, "Ol' Delaney stinks like pigs, E-I-E-I-O!"

Tammy, Kat, and Annie laughed, but my heart tightened. Brooke's teasing was cruel. Didn't anyone else see that?

Eddie rang the bell and told us to load up the buses. I looked down the field and saw Delaney come out from behind the gym. Kat, Annie, Tammy, and Brooke got on the bus, but I waited for Delaney. She was wearing a shirt that said BE PRESENT, and she did smell a little like the ranch. "Do you want some bug spray?" I asked.

"Sure," she said. So I sprayed a lot, and it covered up the stink.

...

Thunder Ridge was much woodsier and more spread out than Star Lake. It was weird to think that there were so many different camps. I bet Star Lake was the prettiest and the best. Even with Brooke there.

A disc jockey was playing music on the tennis courts, and a lot of girls started dancing right away. The Thunder Ridge boys clearly hadn't spent as much time worrying about showering or getting dressed as we had. Most of them were sweaty, and they were wearing regular old shorts and T-shirts. Darby told the six of us that we could get Popsicles in the canteen, dance on the tennis courts, and walk the wooded trails, but that the boys' cabins were off limits. As if I would ever go inside a boys' cabin! Then she said, "Have fun! Don't do anything I wouldn't do!" She winked and headed off toward Todd Casey and the other counselors who were talking in clusters around camp.

"Let's get Popsicles," I suggested.

"No," said Brooke. "The Popsicles will attract mosquitoes. Let's dance. I'm going to meet a boy tonight."

I wanted to say that we'd doused ourselves with bug spray, so we didn't have to worry about mosquitoes. I wanted to say that the boys probably smelled worse than the ranch at camp. I wanted to say that Brooke could do what she wanted, but the rest of us were going to get Popsicles and have our own fun. But Tammy said,

"Yes! Let's find a boyfriend for Brooke!" And Kat and Annie acted as if they'd never heard a better idea in their lives. So they skipped off together, arm in arm in arm in arm, toward the tennis courts.

Tammy turned around and asked, "Are you coming?"

I didn't want to spend my evening finding a boy for Brooke Bernstein. What exactly did she plan to do with the boy once she got him, anyway? Yuck. I didn't want to even think about that. But what was my alternative? Hanging out with Delaney?

"We're getting Popsicles," Delaney said, grabbing my arm and surprising me.

"Have fun!" Brooke called without turning around.

My heart skipped a beat. Was this what I wanted? To be friends with the weird girl? To be left behind? Shouldn't I be with Tammy and the rest of them? Wasn't that where I belonged?

Tammy and I locked eyes for a moment, and I thought it wasn't too late for me to run and catch up with them. But then she turned, and the moment was gone. I wasn't sure what had just happened. Had I chosen Delaney, or had Tammy chosen Brooke? Either way, here I was, stuck with Delaney at a social.

We headed down the path to the canteen. No doubt about it, this was an awkward silence. I wasn't talking, and neither was she. We got cherry Popsicles and sat on a bench near the tennis courts. The music was blaring, and everyone was dancing. I watched Tammy, Brooke,

Kat, and Annie weave through the crowd, point to different boys, and laugh. A counselor tried to get Delaney and me to dance, and we told her we would when we'd finished our Popsicles. I made mine last as long as possible. I licked it so slowly that it melted down my arm. Delaney said, "You want to find a bathroom to wash up?"

Her Popsicle had stained her chapped skin, making the pink ring around her mouth red. She looked like a clown. "Why do you lick your lips all the time?" I asked.

"I don't know. It's a habit, I guess. Why do you compete with Brooke for Tammy's attention all the time?"

"I don't—" I stopped in mid-sentence because I did compete with Brooke. I just wished I didn't. And I wished Delaney hadn't noticed it. "Well, it's a habit, I guess."

Delaney nodded. Then that silence fell again.

Finally Delaney said, "You and Tammy used to be best friends, right?"

"Yes. I mean no. We're *still* best friends."

"Oh. Okay. Sorry." Delaney looked right at me, and it made me uncomfortable. I licked my finger and wiped at the sticky mess on my arm.

"And now Brooke is ruining everything?" she asked.

I nodded.

"That really stinks."

My throat felt all clogged up.

"Well, what are you going to do?"

I shrugged. I thought I might start crying if I tried

to speak. And I wasn't about to do that in front of Delaney.

"Maybe you need to let go a bit," Delaney said thoughtfully. "Step out of the competition and let things fall the way they're meant to fall."

That was terrible advice. Loser's advice. "You mean let Brooke win?"

"No. I mean take a step back. Stop trying so hard, and enjoy the summer." She looked down at her shirt. "Be present."

I bet anything Delaney had never had a best friend. If she had, she'd know you can't give up so easily. Best friends forever meant just that. Forever.

The counselor from before was heading toward us. I really didn't feel like dancing, and my arm was sticky. I stood up. "Let's find a bathroom."

The problem with boys' camps was that there weren't many bathrooms for girls. We were told to go to the office, which was about three million miles away, through wooded trails. It was getting dark out, and we had no idea where we were going. I thought wild animals must be watching us from the forest.

All of a sudden, I heard rustling up ahead. We both stood still. My heart pounded. We tiptoed forward, and I caught my breath. Two figures were standing under a tree. I knew that shaggy hair. It was Todd Casey. And he had his arms around Darby. Whoa! My matchmaking had really worked. They were leaning in for a kiss. Their heads tilted. Their lips touched. And then loud voices from behind us interrupted them.

It was Madison and her friends. Darby and Todd looked up and saw us. Todd ran his hand through his hair, and Darby said, "Hey, girls!" as if we hadn't just caught her lip-locked with the hunkiest guy in all of Wisconsin, maybe even the world.

Madison said, "Laney, what are you doing? Spying on your counselor?"

The other girls laughed, and Delaney said, "We were just looking for the bathroom."

"Sure you were," Madison said, patting Delaney's shoulder in an all-knowing kind of way.

"I'll take you to the bathroom," Darby said.

"That's okay," Madison said. "We're heading there now. We'll take care of these two. See you later!" She smiled really big at Todd, and so did all her friends. I wondered what it must be like for Todd to work at a girls' camp and to know that everyone had a crush on him. And how did Darby feel? She was the lucky one he liked back!

As we walked to the bathroom, Madison quietly told Delaney, "You can't spy on them like that. It's totally uncool. And quit licking your lips. You look ridiculous." Delaney nodded her head quickly, as if she was used to being told what to do by Madison.

I'd always wanted an older sister, someone to pave the way and explain everything to me so I wouldn't make so many mistakes. But I sure didn't want a sister like Madison. I didn't need someone to point out all of my dumb moves.

• • •

Back in our cabin after the social, Annie played her bongos and Kat danced while Tammy and Brooke made up badly rhyming raps about the entire evening.

"Brooke was looking for a guy to kiss,
    But all the boys at Thunder Ridge were wimps."
"Yo, yo, yo, we danced under the moon,
    Till Kat and Annie said 'Va va voom.' "

They laughed so hard at that one that Kat actually wet her pants a little. I obviously missed the joke. It made me realize that even though Delaney might not be as terrible as I'd first thought, I couldn't spend so much time with her if it meant I'd be left out of the group. That night, as I tried to fall asleep, I rubbed Henry's nose so much that I made a hole.

12

On Sunday we slept late and woke up to the sounds of the counselors horseback-riding by the cabins, banging on pots and pans with wooden spoons and announcing that it was Gold Rush Day. The counselors were all dressed up as cowboys and Indians. We ate a Western-style brunch, complete with blueberry pancakes, biscuits and honey, and bacon galore. Then we searched for gold-painted rocks and gambled in the camp casino. Our whole cabin stuck together for most of the day, so at least I didn't feel like I was missing out on anything.

I wasn't the only one who thought it would be cool to be Firelighter. Everyone was talking about who deserved it. And as Kat and Annie told me on the bus, the kids being discussed were mostly the oldest campers. Still, I had to believe Eddie and Maureen were fair-minded people. They'd look at all the campers. And maybe, just maybe, they'd notice a new girl excelling at all her activities (well, except for waterskiing) and dealing very well with some friendship challenges in her cabin. You never knew. It could happen.

That night we were all wearing our yellow Camp Star Lake shirts and blue skirts, and we were waiting outside our cabin for the friendship chain. I heard the girls from Cabin Woods before I saw them. They were singing:

> "Make new friends, but keep the old.
> One is silver and the other gold."

They came up the hill from their special cabin down by the lake, and one by one each cabin joined in the song and the chain. Soon our whole camp, all one hundred campers plus the counselors, were holding hands and walking down the hill toward the fire circle. As we sang the song over and over again, I wondered about the lyrics. Was it really possible to make new friends and keep the old? Or had a grownup written that song? One who didn't remember what it was like to be eleven.

The sky over Star Lake was blushing pink as the sun dipped behind the pine trees on the opposite shore. A cool breeze blew, making the hairs on my arms stand up.

As we took our seats around the fire circle, everyone was quiet, and all I heard was the sounds of the lake lapping against the beach and the buzzing of mosquitoes and crickets. This wasn't like any other evening at camp, when girls laughed and talked and Eddie had to calm us all down. Tonight there was a feeling of anticipation and seriousness in the air. Maybe because we were all dressed alike. Maybe because of the song and the friendship chain. Maybe because of the promise of the Firelighter award. I felt as if anything could happen.

Maureen played her guitar, and the music was soulful and sweet, and I was smiling without even meaning to. Tonight's theme was "Time," and we were urged to make the most of each moment at camp. The girls from Cabin Woods read poems that they wrote about how they couldn't believe this was their last summer as campers. It might be cool to be in Cabin Woods one day. But only if Brooke decided to go to a different camp.

We sang songs — some happy and silly, others touching and bittersweet. The counselors gave out achievement awards for the different activities. Brooke got one for waterskiing. She beamed as she walked to the front and received her award from Darby and Todd. Darby hugged her, then Todd actually put his arm around her back and patted her shoulder. It was just for a quick second, but I would have died if that had been me. He was wearing blue jeans and a yellow polo, and his hair was brushed instead of windblown. I wondered what he smelled like.

Everyone clapped for Brooke, but when she sat back down with us, she seemed more excited about Todd touching her than she was about the award. "He is so slammin' cool!" she whispered. "Darby is the luckiest!"

That morning Delaney and I had told the rest of our cabinmates about the romance blooming between Todd and Darby. Then we'd serenaded Darby with the traditional "Darby and Todd sitting in a tree, K-I-S-S-I-N-G." Darby had laughed good-naturedly, but when we'd asked for details, she'd said that some things were meant to be private, even at camp.

Eddie gave out Sunshine awards to five girls. Kat whispered, "That's kind of like mini-Firelighter. Sunshine Girls are all peppy and smiley and full of camp spirit." The awards were simply yellow squares of paper that said "Sunshine Girl" and the year. But everyone cheered, and the Sunshine Girls beamed, and Maureen took a picture of them with Eddie. Then we all sang, "You Are My Sunshine."

Finally, after the sky turned to a periwinkle blue, it was time to announce the Firelighter. Eddie called a girl named Jennie Cohen from Cabin Woods, the last Firelighter from the summer before. He gave her a flaming birch torch, which she held with two hands. Then he took a piece of paper out of his pocket, unfolded it, and held it up for Jennie to read. Jennie's eyes sparkled. Even though I knew in my head I was not about to be named Firelighter, my body got all fluttery with anticipation and hope.

"This week's Firelighter is a camper who tries her best at every activity," Jennie read. "She can often be found straightening up the boat shed or telling funny stories to her many friends around camp. She has a can-do attitude that inspires all who know her. This week's Firelighter is . . . Madison Reed!"

My heart sank, but I cheered along with everyone else. Madison's whole cabin clobbered her with screams and hugs. Delaney jumped up and ran to congratulate her sister. If Madison were my sister, and if she treated me the way she treated Delaney, I didn't think I'd be so quick to jump on the Madison fan train. I'd probably think the whole thing was unfair. But that was just me. Maybe I wasn't cut out to be Firelighter, after all.

After climbing out from under the mass of hugging girls, Madison made it to the front of the fire circle, where Jennie passed her the torch. Madison, tears in her eyes, lit the bonfire, and we all sang:

"We love you, Madison, oh yes we do.
We don't love anyone as much as you!"

I guess I was happy for Madison, but I was confused, too. Was being rude and bossy to your younger sister considered okay? I doubted that was what they meant by "the character and spirit of Camp Star Lake." Maybe, though, Eddie didn't see everything there was to see.

I noticed Delaney standing to the side, watching her sister. She licked her lips. She wasn't smiling. It looked like she was thinking hard, focusing on something that wasn't even there.

As the bonfire crackled and glowed, we sang songs until the sky was sprinkled with stars. I looked up and saw the Milky Way, like a white rainbow in the night. I squeezed Tammy's hand and pointed. She tilted her head up, and sighed. Then she elbowed Brooke and said "Look" to Kat and Annie. And the five of us stared in awe.

• • •

"I know some of you haven't jibed yet," Nancy said at sailing on Monday. "But today the conditions are perfect for you to try it. There will be a jibe turn in the Star Lake Cup, so if you want to enter it, you'll need to feel comfortable jibing."

Uh-oh. Nancy expected us to do that dangerous turn? I didn't know that would be part of the race.

Delaney raised her hand and asked, "Can you explain jibing again?"

"Sure." Nancy drew a diagram of a boat and an arrow to represent the wind. "Jibing is how you turn the boat when you're sailing downwind." She drew a dotted line to show this movement. "As opposed to coming about, which is a slow and controlled turn *into* the wind, when you jibe, the sail will want to flop over to the other side of the boat very suddenly and sometimes with a great deal of force as you turn *away* from the wind." She drew another boat with the sail on the opposite side. "The first mate can prevent that from happening by pulling the sail in before it would naturally come over."

She put the marker down and looked right at us. "The important thing to remember is you need to control the jibe. An uncontrolled jibe will land you in Star Lake, maybe with a bump on your head from the boom." Nancy raised her eyebrows to see if she'd made herself clear. She had. But she hadn't done anything to make me less afraid.

"Okay, sailors, if there are no more questions, partner up and get on out there. I'll be patrolling in the safety boat, keeping an eye on you."

Tammy touched my shoulder. "I'm going to sail with Brooke today. Okay?"

"Oh," I said, surprised. "But we're sailing together in the Cup, so don't you think we should practice together?"

"Well, yeah, but Brooke asked me already, so . . ."

"So?"

"So, I'm just letting you know. Okay?"

"Fine," I said. "No problem." I didn't get it. We'd had so much fun sailing together on Friday. Why did she want to sail with Brooke now?

Tammy and Brooke headed off to the shed together. I turned to Delaney. "Want to sail with me?"

Delaney said, "Sure," and we hurried into the boat shed to grab life jackets and choose our sail. Brooke and Tammy took the sunset sail. The cotton-candy sail and the preppy sail got taken right away, too. Delaney and I chose the blue-and-gray sail, which reminded me of a shadow. I felt bad for the plain old green sails and yellow sails. Nobody ever wanted those.

The life jacket was cold and wet. I sucked in my stomach so it didn't touch me until I got more used to it. We stepped carefully over the smooth rocks at the shoreline, waded into Star Lake, and rigged our boat. Delaney had the same focused look on her face that she had when she practiced yoga, and we were rigged and sailing away from camp before anyone else had even hoisted a sail.

"Wow," I said. "You really do take after your sister." We headed straight out on a port tack, which meant the wind was coming over the port side of the boat. I was the first mate; I liked being in charge of the sail.

Delaney sighed. "She's better than I am at everything, though."

"Everything?"

"Yes. And she doesn't let me forget it." Delaney steered us a little bit away from the wind, and I let the sail out.

I thought about last night at Fireside, when Madison got Firelighter and Delaney had that faraway look in her eyes. "It must be hard, having to follow in her footsteps."

"It is. That's why I do yoga. Madison never had any interest in it. And it's something my mom and I can share."

"That's cool." For the first time, I saw Delaney's yoga as something other than weird. "I never met a kid who liked yoga before. I thought of it as something for moms, or hippies."

Delaney laughed.

"I mean, don't get me wrong, it's great for you, but personally, I like to be more active. That's why I play soccer and swim. I like feeling out of breath and pushing my body to the limit."

"Well, I do that in yoga."

"Really?"

"Yeah, but there's this very calm force at work, too. It's peaceful. Kind of like this." She swept her arm to the side, as if the whole lake was hers.

The truth was, sailing with Delaney was peaceful. I wasn't worried about whether or not she liked me. I wasn't thinking about winning her friendship or winning a race. I was just enjoying the beauty of the lake. The cool breeze. The warm sun. The sound of the boat slicing through the water.

"Are you ready to try that jibe turn?" Delaney asked.

"Ready as I'll ever be." Actually, I was scared to death. But I wasn't going to let that stop me.

Delaney pointed the boat more toward camp, and the wind blew from behind us. I remembered that point of sail was called running because we were running away from the wind. "Jibe ho!" Delaney shouted.

My heart pounded as I pulled the mainsheet in and Delaney pushed the tiller away from the sail. The boat turned slowly and then suddenly picked up speed as it finished. We ducked, and the boom swung to our side of the boat. The hull dipped into the water, getting our bottoms wet, but we scooched to the other side to even the weight. The mainsheet tugged against my grip, and I let it slide through my fingers just a bit. I blew out a breath. Whew! We did it. "Yes!" I said. "That was way easier than I thought it would be!"

"It sure was. But the wind is awfully light today. I'd hate to jibe on a gusty day."

I thought about the big storm on Friday night when the wind had blown the canoe up the hill. Nobody would sail in weather like that, I thought. Still, it wouldn't hurt to practice some more. "Let's try it again."

13

Dear Mom, Dad, and Derek,

It's hard to believe I've been at camp for only nine days. It feels much longer than that. But in a good way. It's just that so much has happened already. I've learned to sail. And to ride a horse. And in gymnastics, I'm working on my back walkover. Nobody takes soccer very seriously here, but it's fun anyway. Swimming laps in a lake is much harder than in the pool, but I'm practicing all my strokes.

Waterskiing is the only activity I'm having trouble with. I still can't get up no matter how hard I try. But I get to ride in the boat with my counselor Darby and the boat driver, Todd. I think Darby and Todd are in love!

Some of the cabin groups left for overnighters

today, but not us. You don't find out where you're going until the day before you leave. Eddie makes you go on a treasure hunt to figure out your destination. Last year, Kat and Annie's cabin went to the Dells where they got to ride awesome waterslides. And there's a rumor that one year Cabin Woods went to Disney World. But I doubt that's true.

xoxoxoxoxox to infinity, Jemma

I didn't tell my family about what was going on between Tammy and me because if I didn't understand it, how could I explain it to them? It was as if Brooke had Tammy under some kind of spell. Deep inside, though, Tammy still had to be Tammy. Maybe my best bet was to remind her of who she really was and of what our friendship was all about. I could do that.

Tuesday at dinner, I entertained our cabin with stories about Tammy and me from when we were little. I had them rolling in laughter when I told them that when Tammy's mom baked cookies, we used to lick the spoons and spatulas clean and put them right back in the silverware drawer.

Tammy said, "I never did that!"

"Yes, you did. We both did."

Kat said, "Jemma has as many stories about growing up with Tammy as I have about Annie and me."

I shrugged and smiled.

Brooke said, "Yeah, but she's making half of them up."

"No I'm not. I just have a really good memory."

Tammy sighed. "I don't know. We'd have to ask my mom to verify that one."

I couldn't believe Tammy didn't remember. It had happened, and more than once, too. But the point wasn't to fight with Tammy. It was to get her to remember the good times, to snap her out of her fascination with Brooke and come back to me. So I let it go.

Wednesday morning during cabin cleanup, Brooke was homesick again. I thought that if she would just open all those letters, she might not be so sad. Maybe whatever was in those letters would help Brooke. Then she wouldn't be so dependent on Tammy, and Tammy wouldn't have to be so protective of her. Wouldn't Brooke's curiosity make her at least peek at one of the letters? I wished I could read them, and they weren't even mine.

Brooke was on her bed, pouting, and Tammy was comforting her. So I swept the floor for Tammy, even though it was her job.

That night when canteen opened, I bought Tammy a Take Five, her favorite candy bar. "What's this for?" she asked.

"No reason," I said. "I just saw the Take Five and thought of you."

Brooke rolled her eyes, but Tammy said, "Thanks, Jemma. That was so sweet of you."

"If you're trying to win Firelighter," Brooke said, "you should wait until a counselor is around before you do all these nice things."

I glared at Brooke. "I'm not trying to *win* Firelighter. Jeez!" Sweat trickled down the back of my neck. Was wanting to be Firelighter the same thing as trying to win it? If so, then I bet almost all the campers were guilty. But this wasn't even about Firelighter. This was about Tammy. "Haven't you ever heard of friends doing nice things for each other for no reason?"

"Whatever," she said.

I looked at Tammy, hoping she'd come to my defense, but she had a mouth full of chocolate.

On Thursday we had a luau, and Tammy, Brooke, and I were making flower leis at the picnic tables. Brooke left to go to the bathroom, and Eddie came by and admired our work. "Those are beautiful," he said. "Hey, Erikson, where's your other half?"

For a second I didn't know what he was talking about. Other half of her lei? But then he said, "Oh, here she is." And I saw that he meant Brooke, who was just returning from the bathroom. Why didn't he say, Where's the third musketeer? or something like that? Was it that obvious to everyone that Brooke and Tammy were best friends, and I was the lowly tagalong?

I remembered that in fourth grade Ellyn Eiden called Tammy and me Jemmy Erikman, combining both our names because we were so close. I wanted to remind Tammy of that right now, but I couldn't bring myself to start yet another "Remember when" conversation with her. I was beginning to understand that a friendship couldn't survive on memories alone.

• • •

Before I knew it, it was Sunday again—this time Pirate Day—and Darby told us at brunch that our cabin had been asked to present a cabin thought at Fireside. So after we ate and before the treasure hunt and water activities for Pirate Day began, we sat in the sun on the hill and tossed ideas around. Tonight's theme for Fireside was "Better Together."

Kat said, "Let's be creative. We can do an interpretive dance showing the power of togetherness." She pulled Annie up and they twirled and leaped around our circle to demonstrate.

Brooke said, "I do believe that will turn out to be the Kat and Annie show."

"Yes! A sneak peek of the talent show," Kat said, beaming.

"But this isn't the talent show," Tammy said. "This is Fireside."

"Tammy's right," I said. "What about a poem?"

"No, that's boring," Brooke said. "Besides, that's what Woods did last week."

"What if we speak from the heart?" Delaney offered. "We can each answer the question 'How are we better together?'"

"Boring," Brooke declared in a singsong voice.

She sure had an easy time knocking all our ideas down. But I didn't hear her coming up with any of her own. We'd be "better together" without Brooke Bernstein, that was for sure. "Well, what do you suggest, Brooke?" I asked.

"I happen to have the perfect idea," Brooke said. "We can pair off and act out scenes of someone trying to do something alone and succeeding only when her partner comes along to help. Like, I could pretend to be practicing my tennis serve, but every time I hit the ball, I have to run to the other side of the court to get the ball to try it again. Then Tammy shows up with her racket and says, 'I'll play with you.' And then we pretend to have a rally going back and forth. Kat and Annie can do something else that shows it. And so can you and Delaney. Then we all say, 'Good alone, but better together!' What do you think?"

"I like it," Tammy said.

Figured. She liked everything Brooke said. Kat and Annie nodded their heads in agreement. Delaney was the only one who seemed unconvinced. She squinted at Brooke and licked her lips.

"Then we agree, right?" Brooke said. "We each just have to come up with our mini-skits."

But I wasn't convinced, either. "Wait a second," I said. "Better together. Not better in pairs. It's not about pairing off. It's about being together as a cabin. A whole cabin."

"What's the difference?" Brooke asked.

"There's a huge difference," I said. "When you pair off, you leave people out."

"No you don't. Not when there's an even number. Two and two and two. Everyone's included."

How was I supposed to argue with that logic? I knew how to divide by two. And lately I'd been partnering off more and more with Delaney. We'd sailed together all week. It had been fun, but did that mean I didn't feel left out when Brooke and Tammy paired off? Of course not. "Still," I said. "I think we should do something with all six of us."

Delaney nodded. "That sounds better to me," she said.

"Well, let's vote on it," Brooke said. "All those who like my idea, raise your hands." Brooke, Kat, and Annie raised their hands. Tammy mouthed the word "Sorry" to me and raised hers, too. "Four to two. I win." Brooke smiled smugly.

I'd have liked to wipe that smile right off her face. I sat on my hands to make sure I didn't do anything I'd regret.

"Hold on," Delaney said. "If we're going to pair off, it makes sense that we each do what we want to do. So Kat and Annie should do their expressive dance. You and Tammy can do your skit. And Jemma and I will speak from the heart with a poem about togetherness."

"That's perfect!" Kat and Annie said at the same time. Then Kat snorted, and we all laughed.

All but Brooke, that is. She said, "I don't know. I don't think we'll look unified that way."

"Don't worry," Delaney said. "Jemma and I will go last, and our poem will tie it all together. Right, Jemma?"

"Right!" I said. And at that moment I began to really like Delaney Reed.

• • •

At Fireside, we all sang "We Go Together," from *Grease* and listened to a song by Jack Johnson called "Better Together." I'd never heard the Jack Johnson song before, and I loved the way it sounded. Especially the part about how words can't even express how much better we are together. I looked at Tammy during that part of the song. Our eyes met for a moment, and we smiled, and I thought that maybe all my jealousy and insecurity was ridiculous.

Eddie called us up for our cabin thought. Kat and Annie did their dance, Tammy and Brooke did their skit, and then Delaney and I read our poem:

"What does together look like?
Is it one hundred girls singing around a campfire?
Six girls in a cabin, coming up with one thought?
Five girls on a basketball team?
Four girls playing doubles tennis?
Three girls creating a dance?
Two girls sailing a boat?
One girl practicing yoga?
Or is it the whole world, living together in
peace?
Sharing ideas, sharing thoughts, sharing
friendship and love . . .
We are all better together."

I wasn't so sure about the one-girl-practicing-yoga line. I mean, how was that together? But Delaney said she felt connected with the whole wide planet when she did yoga.

Everyone applauded after we finished the poem, so I guessed it worked. I squeezed Delaney's hand. She licked her lips and grinned at me.

Eddie gave out the achievement awards, and this time Kat got one for hip-hop. Annie got one for music. And Delaney got one for sailing. "Congratulations!" I said after Delaney sat down with her sailing award.

"Thanks!" Delaney smiled wider than I'd seen all summer. I looked at her three-inch-square piece of red paper. There was a picture of a sailboat and the words "Outstanding Achievement in Sailing at Camp Star Lake." That was it. But she was holding it in her hands as if it were a rare jewel. I knew I'd be holding mine the exact same way if I'd gotten one.

The Sunshine awards were given out, and my name was not called. Tammy and I were the only ones in our cabin who hadn't received any award at all this summer. What if one of us got Firelighter? Right now. It was a long shot, I knew. But anything was possible. And I really wanted it to be me.

Madison got up and held the burning birch torch. Eddie unfolded the paper for her. I watched her eyes scan to the bottom of the paper to see the name of the lucky girl. A huge smile spread across Madison's face. Would she have smiled that way if my name was on that paper? "This week's Firelighter has been a camper for six years," she started.

I didn't really hear the rest. My disappointment pushed all the good feelings from Fireside away. I wished I didn't care so much about that dumb award. But I did. I didn't even know why. A girl from Cabin Woods, Dani Schwachman, was named Firelighter, and I cheered and sang along with everyone else, even though my heart wasn't in it. If I were a better person, if I truly deserved to be the Firelighter, I wouldn't have these jealous feelings at all.

When Fireside ended and we were walking back

up the hill to our cabin, Madison found us in the dark. "Hey, congrats on your sailing award," she said to Delaney.

"Thanks."

"I got one my first summer, too."

"I know."

Why couldn't Madison let Delaney enjoy her award without pointing out that she'd also gotten one? Delaney deserved a sister who would support her, not compete with her. I said, "Delaney really earned the sailing award. She helped me so much this week. It's hard to believe she's just a beginner."

"Really?"

"Yes." And then an idea shot out of my mouth. "You should sail with her in the Star Lake Cup. You guys should be partners. And if you win, your nickname on the Cup could be Sailing Sisters!" As I said this, I realized how dumb it was. If Delaney and Madison really did sail together, they would be impossible to beat, and I was still hoping to win the Cup with Tammy. But it was clear from the horrified look on both of their faces that I didn't have to worry about that.

Madison laughed and said, "I'm not about to sail with a sixth grader."

And Delaney said, "Yeah. No, thank you!"

"It was just an idea," I said.

"Besides, Lisa and I are planning to repeat our victory this year," Madison said. "So if either of you is thinking about entering the race, I wish you lots of luck. You're gonna need it." She smiled and waved at us as she entered her cabin. "Have a good night!"

The screen door slammed, and Delaney flinched. We didn't say anything more as we walked the rest of the way to our cabin.

14

The whiteboard was out again at sailing on Monday, and the words Triangle Race Course were printed across the top. "So, girls," Nancy said, "here we are with less than two weeks until the Star Lake Cup. It's time to get cracking. If you haven't tried a jibe turn yet, I suggest you work on that today. I'll have the sign-up sheet for the race posted in the boat shed, so if you plan to enter, you need to find a partner and sign up as soon as possible.

"We will be racing a triangle course. This is a basic kind of race that requires you to maneuver your boat around three buoys." She drew the buoys on the board along with arrows showing the direction in which we'd have to sail. "Everything you've been working on this summer will be tested in the race. If you look out at Star

Lake, you'll see I've set up a practice course. These buoys will be in place until the end of camp, and you'll be able to practice during class time as well as during open period. Any questions?"

I raised my hand. "What if there are more sailors than there are boats?"

"Well, I can always bring in extra boats for the day. That's why I have you sign up in advance. I need to know how many boats to have."

Brooke asked, "Is it really fair to have us beginners race against the older girls? Shouldn't we have a Star Lake Cup Junior or something?"

Nancy shook her head and smiled. "I told you on the first day we met that you would know everything you needed to know to compete. Some of you will choose not to enter this year, and that's fine. But if you work hard and do your very best, I believe it's possible the Cup could be engraved with two of your names."

I felt all fluttery and light, imagining Tammy and me winning the Cup. We would each hold one of the handles and lift the trophy over our heads as the rest of the camp applauded. Eddie would snap our picture and maybe put it in the brochure. I elbowed Tammy and gave her the thumbs-up sign. She smiled back at me, but she didn't look very confident. We'd have to start practicing. We hadn't sailed together since that time we learned to capsize. And today I'd already agreed to "hike out" with Delaney. That's when you pulled the mainsheet in tight to make the boat tilt up on an angle. Then you leaned your body all the way out of the boat to keep it from capsizing. I'd seen older campers do it last week and thought it looked like a blast.

It was windy today, and Delaney and I rigged the shadow boat and got going right away. Delaney pointed us on a beam reach, which meant we were sailing perpendicular to the wind. We were moving pretty fast, and I pulled the sail in tighter to make the boat lift up. "Whoa!" Delaney said, and she moved the tiller starboard, pointing us closer to the wind. The boat flattened out.

"No," I said. "Keep us going like before. It feels awesome."

"Okay." She pointed us back away from the wind, and again the boat tilted up. We braced our feet in the cockpit and straightened our legs so our butts were sticking out the side of the boat.

"Woo-hoo!" I cried. "This is great!" I felt like we were going a hundred miles an hour. The water sprayed up at us, and we leaned all the way out of the boat, which was just shy of capsizing.

I held on to the mainsheet to keep myself from falling out of the boat, but poor Delaney just gripped the tiller with one hand and the edge of the boat with the other. "Ahhh!" she yelled.

We both laughed and laughed, and before long the water and the laughter worked their magic on me. "I have to pee!" I said.

Delaney laughed even harder. "Me too!"

"Let's do it."

And so there we were, two eleven-year-olds, peeing off the side of a Sunfish boat in the middle of Star Lake, laughing our heads off.

Afterward we let the boat even out, and I said, "That is definitely the most fun way to sail."

"For sure." Delaney took a deep breath. Then she said, "You know how you said I should sail in the Cup with my sister?"

"Yeah?"

"Well, I was thinking I'd really like to sail in it with you."

"Oh. Well, I would, you know, but Tammy and I already said we'd be partners."

"Really?"

I nodded, but Delaney looked like she didn't believe me. "What?" I asked.

"It's just, aren't Tammy and Brooke partners?"

"No. Tammy and I talked about it the first week of camp."

"And you don't think she's changed her mind since then?"

She couldn't have changed her mind. She wouldn't have. At least not without telling me. I looked out at all the other sailboats on the lake. Tammy was in one of them with Brooke right now. I wasn't even sure which one. What if they were planning to sail in the race together?

Delaney looked at me doubtfully. She didn't understand. "I know it seems crazy," I told her. "And I really do have so much fun sailing with you. But Tammy and I already agreed to partner up. So . . ."

"I get it," Delaney said. "It's fine."

I didn't know who Delaney would find to partner with for the Cup. I hoped she would find someone. I wanted Madison to see how good she really was.

• • •

I had to check with Tammy about the race, but I needed to find a time when it was just her and me, and that wasn't easy. Brooke was always around.

Tuesday at ranching, after we'd fed all the animals and cleaned out their pens, Mallory asked for volunteers to take Wayne, the Shetland pony, for a walk. "We'll do it!" I said. "Right, Tam?"

Tammy nodded, and Mallory warned us before we set off to hold tight to Wayne's lead rope.

"Hey, Wayne, my man," Tammy said, rubbing the soft part of his nose, "where to?" Wayne bobbed his head up and down. "I think he wants to take a tour of Camp Star Lake."

"And we'll be his lovely tour guides. On your left,

Wayne, you'll see the gym, second home of Kat and Annie O'Reilly." I gestured like a flight attendant pointing out the exits, and Tammy laughed.

We walked past the gym and over to the tennis courts, where we were greeted by the sounds of balls bouncing and gym shoes shuffling.

"Keep that horse off the courts!" a counselor called to us as she fed balls to a line of girls practicing their forehands.

Tammy raised her eyebrows at me in a way that said, Oops!

"So inhospitable!" I said. "Don't you worry, Wayne. Most CSL counselors are friendlier than that. Let's head down to the stables so Wayne can meet his big brothers."

"Do Shetland ponies and horses get along?" Tammy asked.

I shrugged. "Why wouldn't they?"

"Off we go, then," Tammy said, and she led Wayne around the front of the Lodge and down the hill. He stopped every few steps to nibble on the clover that grew in the grass.

I didn't think I would ever get tired of this view. Girls were swimming, skiing, sailing, and wakeboarding. But even with all that activity, the lake shone with a calming force. "Straight ahead, you'll see beautiful Star Lake, home to the most glorious sunsets known to mankind," I told Wayne in my tour guide voice.

Tammy sighed and said, "Seriously. Isn't it just amazing here, Jem? I never knew I could love a place so much. I never even thought about it."

"I know what you mean." As we passed the boating shed on our way to the riding ring, I thought about mentioning the Cup, but I didn't have the words yet. How was I supposed to ask Tammy about something she'd already agreed to without sounding insecure?

When we approached the stables, Wayne stopped and made a funny sound.

"Oh, look, the poor thing is scared," I said. "You don't have to be scared of the big horsies, Wayne. Come on." I patted his behind, and Tammy pulled on his lead rope. He took a few hesitant steps closer to the fence. Eight girls were trotting figure eights in the riding ring. Wayne stopped again.

"Maybe this isn't such a good idea," Tammy said.

"Maybe not." Wayne stomped his front leg. Just then one of the horses neighed and reared up on his hind legs. The girl on that horse screamed. Wayne bucked, and the rope flew out of Tammy's hands.

Wayne ran like crazy.

"No!" Tammy and I both yelled, and we chased after him.

Wayne galloped up the hill. Tammy and I followed. He ran through a soccer game and across the softball field. The softball counselor yelled at us while all the girls laughed. He ran past archery and arts and crafts.

He crossed the gooney birds at the camp's entrance and ran into the woods. I had no idea where he was headed. The distance between us grew, and branches scratched at my legs as I tried to keep up. Wayne had serious stamina.

Finally we came into a clearing. We were at the ranch. We had come around the back way. I prayed that Mallory was in the barn or someplace where she wouldn't see Wayne before we got there. He came to a halt at the duck pond, stuck his head in, and drank. The ducks made a ruckus and escaped the pond. Mallory came out of the barn. "Hey, what's going on?" she asked.

"Nothing," we said at the same time.

"Wayne's thirsty, that's all," I offered, panting.

"Well, take him over to his water trough," Mallory said. "The girls just refilled it." She walked back into the barn, and Tammy and I both fell to the ground in exhaustion and relief.

"Oh my God," Tammy said. Then she looked at me, and at the same time we both burst out laughing.

My stomach went up and down, up and down, as I tried to catch my breath. I looked at the blue sky dotted with small white, puffy clouds. And then suddenly I realized that Tammy and I had created a new memory for this summer. And that realization gave me the courage to bring up the Cup. "Tam, I was thinking about the Star Lake Cup. And I think we should really spend some time sailing together if we want to have a chance to win it. You know?"

Tammy bit her lower lip. "Jemma, I thought you were going to sail with Delaney." She propped herself up on an elbow, and I did the same.

My heart pounded, and my stomach flipped. I didn't know what to say. Had I been fooling myself all summer? I got a flash of the look Delaney had given me when I told her I was going to sail with Tammy. Maybe it hadn't been misunderstanding in her eyes. Maybe it had been pity. Maybe she'd felt sorry for poor, dumb Jemma, the last girl to figure out her best friend had completely ditched her.

"You said we were going to sail together." I fought to keep my voice steady.

"Yeah, but that was so long ago."

"No it wasn't. Not really." I blinked back tears.

Tammy sighed. "I'm so sorry, Jemma, but I told Brooke—"

"What could you tell Brooke? You made a commitment to me that time we capsized together. Remember?"

"Okay. I'm sorry. You're right. Can you just let me think about it? Please?"

I couldn't talk anymore. I felt sick. I realized letting her think about it was better than an out-and-out no. So I nodded.

15

I was too embarrassed to tell Delaney about my conversation with Tammy. The next day at sailing I decided to head off any suspicions right away. "Tammy and I are going to practice during open period, so you and I can sail together in class today."

"Oh good," she said. "Let's hike out again."

We chose the shadow sail, and I checked the Cup sign-up sheet as I slipped into my life jacket. So far, three pairs had signed up: Madison and Lisa; Elle and Samantha, eighth graders I knew from my riding class; and Leah and Zoey, two sixth graders from Cabin Five. I wanted my name up there on that list with Tammy. But even more, I wanted Tammy to want that, too. Because if she didn't want to be my partner, maybe I didn't want to be hers, either.

Delaney and I sailed together easily. I began to anticipate her movements, and she mine. But I couldn't truly enjoy myself. I kept looking at Tammy and Brooke in the cotton-candy boat. I kept wishing.

"Is everything okay?" Delaney asked.

I let my fingers trail in the lake and watched the water rush around them. "I'm just tired."

• • •

Since I'd lied about sailing with Tammy during open period, I had to hide when that time came. Delaney usually practiced yoga in the cabin or hung out at the ranch then, so I stayed away from that part of camp. It made the most sense to go down to the riding ring, because that was at least in the same direction as the sailing dock. But I couldn't ride in a swimsuit, and I wouldn't look like I'd been sailing if I was wearing jeans and boots. So I settled on swimming laps. If Delaney wondered why I was so wet, I could always tell her that we'd capsized.

At the swimming dock, there was a group of girls sunbathing, and some others playing in the lake. I said hi, then checked in with Gina, the swimming counselor, before I hopped in. I loved the water. I loved the muffled sound of nothingness when I was under, and I loved the feel of the sun on my face when I came up for air. I started off with freestyle. Stroke, stroke, stroke, breathe. Stroke, stroke, stroke, breathe. After a while I didn't think about it. My body just fell into a soothing rhythm of strokes and breaths, strokes and breaths. Soon my mind got to that empty space where there was nothing. Nothing but me, my breath, the water, the air. I did freestyle, backstroke, breaststroke, and butterfly before I was totally spent. I climbed out and wrapped myself in my towel. Then I chatted with the sunbathing girls for a bit before I headed up to my cabin.

As soon as the screen door banged behind me, I realized I hadn't thought this lie through properly. Delaney was doing a headstand against the wall. And Tammy and Brooke were in the middle of a conversation about the tennis game they had just finished playing. So much for my charade.

"Hey," I said, thinking it had to be better to pretend everything was normal. "What's up?"

Delaney didn't reply, but then again, she never talked while she was practicing yoga. Tammy said, "Brooke and I were just going to head to the shower house. We're so sweaty from tennis. You want to come?"

"Sure," I said.

While I showered, I tried to come up with a logical way to explain why Tammy was at tennis when I was supposedly sailing with her. But I couldn't think of anything. I just felt embarrassed and ashamed.

On the way to dinner, I still didn't know what to say, but I knew I had to say something. "Delaney," I started. "I . . ." She looked at me as we walked across the field. "I want to explain about . . . I mean . . . well . . . what I'm trying to say is . . ."

Delaney stopped walking and put her hand on my shoulder. "Jemma, don't worry about it. Okay?"

I felt like a bird was flapping its wings inside my chest. "Really?"

"Really. It's fine. I get it."

And the way she looked at me made me believe she really did get it, maybe even more than I did.

• • •

That night at canteen, I bought a cherry-flavored ChapStick for Delaney. "I thought you might like this," I told her. "It'll protect your lips and maybe help you stop licking them. That is, if you want to stop, I mean."

Delaney laughed. "Of course I want to. It's an awful habit. Thanks."

"No problem." I knew a gift of ChapStick couldn't equal what Delaney had given me today, but it was something.

• • •

I kept waiting for Tammy to get back to me about the Star Lake Cup. Wednesday turned to Thursday, and Thursday turned to Friday, and she never mentioned a thing. We both pretended there was nothing hanging unfinished between us. I had to remind myself that we'd really had that conversation Tuesday at ranching, that I really was waiting to see if Tammy would choose me or Brooke. I understood now that the choice meant more than who would be partners for the race. It meant everything. Maybe that's why we both stayed away from the topic.

Friday after lunch, I had to wipe the table, so I was the last one back to our cabin for rest hour. I walked into a familiar scene: Kat and Annie working on a dance, Tammy and Brooke playing Spit, and Delaney practicing yoga. "I'll play winner," I said sitting down next to Tammy and Brooke on the scuffed wood floor.

"That might take a while," Tammy said.

Then I realized they weren't playing Spit. They were playing War Madness.

"Orry-say," Brooke said in pig Latin, and she and Tammy laughed.

I felt as if I'd swallowed a bowling ball. War Madness belonged to Tammy and me.

Brooke threw down a jack and Tammy turned over a king. "Ha! That's three! Gotcha again. Jemma, help me think of a good punishment for Brooke."

Brooke groaned. "Oh-ay oh-nay!"

"I'm sure you can think of one on your own," I said, and I went over to my bed and pulled out my stationery box, certain that the whole cabin could hear my heart beating.

Dear Mom, Dad, and Derek,

I stopped. I left the marker on the page, and my comma turned into a big, inky dot. Kat and Annie kept playing the same section of a Beyoncé song over and over as they tried to figure out the right moves for their special dance, which they were going to do for the Talent Show in five days. All I had to do for the show was a simple gymnastics routine, and I was pretty much ready.

"I can't do that turn!" Annie complained.

"Yes you can, it's easy." Kat did the turn herself. It was some kind of jumpy, twisty thing where she landed on one foot with her other leg pointed directly behind her. "See?"

"I'm not doing it." Annie crossed her arms.

"You're just scared. Come on, come on."

"Shut up already!" Annie stopped the music and stood with her hands on her hips. Strands of her hair had fallen out of her ponytail, and she blew them away from her face. Everyone, even Delaney, looked at her. "I'm not doing the turn, and I'm not doing the dance. I'm not scared. I just don't want to do it. Okay?"

"But—"

"You're the dancer, Kat!" And with that she grabbed her bongos and stormed out of the cabin.

Instantly Kat started to cry. I jumped off my bed to comfort her. Tammy and Brooke stopped their game, and Delaney came out of her pose. We all crowded around Kat, patting her back, asking her if she was okay. After a minute, Kat sniffled and wiped her eyes. "We're

133

both dancers," she said. "I don't know what she's talking about."

It was true, they both danced well. But Kat danced with more than just her body. Her spirit was in every move she made. And with Annie, now that I thought about it, that was never the case. Annie must have realized that, too, yet she kept on dancing. Until now.

"I'm gonna find her," Kat said, getting up. "I'm sure she was just in a bad mood or something."

"Want us to come with you?" Tammy asked.

"No, no, we'll be fine."

The screen door banged behind Kat, and the four of us just looked at one another for a moment. I think we were all surprised that Kat and Annie could disagree, let alone misunderstand each other.

"I'm going outside," Delaney said, rolling up her mat. Tammy and Brooke sat back down by their cards. I didn't want to write a letter anymore. And I certainly didn't want to watch those two play War Madness. So I followed Delaney outside. I sat on our cabin steps, and I watched her do a series of movements. She started out standing up straight, with her hands in a prayer position at her heart. Then she swept her arms up toward the sky before bending down to touch her toes. Her hands came up to her shins and she straightened her back. Then she jumped out into a push-up position before rocking back into an upside-down V. She held that pose for a while, stretching out her calves. Then she jumped forward, straightened up, and started again. She did this whole thing over and over, and each time I had the strangest urge to join her.

After her fifth repetition, Delaney stopped and said, "It's called a Sun Salutation. Want to try?"

Yoga was not my thing. I didn't know how to do it. I'd probably look ridiculous, not graceful and powerful like Delaney. But there I was, standing up and saying okay. Delaney smiled, a huge smile. "But I'm not going to meditate," I said.

Delaney laughed. "Of course not."

So we spent the rest of the hour doing yoga. And I liked it.

• • •

That afternoon, Delaney and I sailed together again, but we didn't do the practice course. There was no need to, since we weren't going to race together. We just enjoyed the lake and each other. I shared some of my waterskiing fiascos with her, and she told me about her troubles with horseback riding, including getting on one horse that refused to move and another one that decided to canter when Delaney didn't even know how to trot. We sang songs, and splashed each other, and even capsized on purpose. I considered for a minute the idea of racing in the Star Lake Cup with Delaney. Telling Tammy to forget it, that she'd lost her chance, that Delaney and I were going to be partners. That would be the safest thing—dumping Tammy before she had a chance to dump me. But then I'd never know for sure what Tammy would have done. What if she'd been planning to choose me all along, and she was just trying to figure out how to let Brooke down gently? Then I'd mess everything up. So, no, it was better to wait and see.

Afterward, when we were putting away our sail, I checked the sign-up sheet in the boat shed. There were eight pairs of racers now, but no Tammy or Brooke. I still had hope.

• • •

Saturday, after another unsuccessful skiing class where the highlight for me was seeing Todd and Darby hold hands in the boat, I headed up to the cabin to change. As I walked in, Brooke was walking out. Today she'd lifted a ski without a problem. That was the first step before dropping one ski and slaloming. I couldn't believe she was practically skiing around the lake on one foot, and I still hadn't gotten up on two. Brooke was wearing the shirt she'd worn on the bus, the hand-made I ♥ CAMP STAR LAKE one. I hadn't worn mine since that day. Last week I pulled it out of my cubby and almost put it on, but then I noticed that the heart wasn't right. It was lopsided and off-center. I wondered if maybe that was why it was mine. I pictured Tammy and Brooke at the Eriksons' kitchen table, the fabric markers spread out in front of them. Did Brooke say, "Oh, shoot, I messed up the heart"? And then did Tammy say, "Here's a new shirt. You can start over, and we can give that one to Jemma"?

Maybe Tammy really did like Brooke more than me.

I looked at Tammy and Brooke's bunk bed. The leis we made the other day were hanging from the bedpost. Brooke's stationery box was on her bed, and her wet towel was on the floor. We'd get points deducted from inspection because of that. I picked up her towel and hung it outside on the clothesline. Then I tried to shove her stationery box back into her cubby, but her cubby was crowded with clothes, and it wasn't an easy fit. While I moved some things around, I happened to touch one of the mystery letters.

I pulled it out and examined it. The return address said "Robert Bernstein." So that was her dad's name. Hmm. I wondered what he was like. What could he have done to make Brooke so angry that she wouldn't even open his mail?

My heart was racing, but I wasn't doing anything wrong. I was just looking at the envelope. Still, I listened carefully to make sure nobody was coming. And then, without thinking, I slid my finger under the flap. Just a tiny bit. I could have stopped. I should have stopped.

But I didn't. With shaky hands, I opened the letter. And I read.

Dear Brooke,

Honey, I know you're angry with me, and I understand. You have every right to be. I truly regret that you found out about Jill the way you did. Sometimes grownups make mistakes. (I seem to have made more than my share this year.) I'm not perfect, and I know I haven't been the best father (and certainly not the best husband), but I hope you will someday find it in your heart to forgive me. Even though your mom and I could not work things out, I will always be your dad, and I will always love you.

Love, Dad

Wow. I couldn't be sure who Jill was, but my guess was she was someone Brooke's dad had a relationship with. Yikes. No wonder Brooke was mad. I tried to imagine getting a letter like this from my own dad. Could he ever cheat on Mom? I didn't think so. But what if he did?

I'd hate him. It'd be like he'd cheated on me, on our whole family. Poor Brooke. Her dad had ruined everything. Even though I already knew her parents were getting divorced, this letter made it seem more real to me. Uglier.

Tammy must have known all of this.

I reread the letter, alert to any sound of someone coming. The thing was, once I got past the shock, I thought the letter was actually nice. He was trying to make up. If only Brooke would read it, she would know. And maybe she wouldn't be so sad, and Tammy wouldn't have to protect her so much, and Brooke wouldn't be so mean to me, and everything would be better.

I was tempted to look at the rest of the letters, but all of a sudden the bell rang, and I jumped. Shoot! I had to get to ranching, and I was still in my swimsuit, and oh my God! I had just opened Brooke's private mail!

My hands shook as I folded the letter back the way it was and jammed it in the envelope. I tried licking the seal and pressing down, but it didn't stick. Oh, no! What had I done? Should I throw the evidence away? What if Brooke knew exactly how many letters there were? And what if she decided to read them at some point? She should get to read this one. Dumb, Jemma! Dumb! Dumb! Dumb!

Okay, calm down. Think. Breathe, I told myself.

I took a few deep breaths, then put the letter in Brooke's cubby. I shoved it way, way back. Maybe, if she ever looked at the letter, she'd think it accidentally got opened from being squished in the back of her cubby. It was possible.

I quickly got dressed and headed to ranching. Nobody ever had to know.

16

A miracle occurred that day. We won inspection! Well, actually, we tied with Cabin Three, but since they'd been Neat Guys about a billion times already this summer, Eddie let us eat first, and he said we'd get to work canteen all by ourselves. We all high-fived each other. I almost told everyone how I'd saved us by cleaning up after Brooke, but then I thought about reading her mail, and my stomach turned over. Besides, Kat seemed to think we won because of her. "See, Annie," she said, "I told you we'd do it, and I cleaned extra hard today. I was on toilet duty and I didn't just flush, I actually used that detergent and scrubbed!" After their big fight yesterday they must have talked and come to an understanding, because they were as tight as ever.

We got in line for lunch: tacos and burritos. And we all started planning for canteen. "I call popcorn," Annie said.

"Slushies!" Brooke announced.

"Soda fountain!" Kat claimed.

"I want to do the Slushies!" I said.

"Let's all take turns," Tammy suggested.

Nobody could argue with that.

During rest hour, Kat and Annie made up a work chart, dividing the assignments so that everyone would get a turn with every job. "You never know," Annie said. "This might be our one and only chance to run canteen."

We were all in great moods at dinner, but when Darby gave us our mail, there was another letter from Brooke's dad in the pile. Just glancing at it made me sweat. I wondered if my face showed my guilt. I wondered if anyone suspected I'd read Brooke's private mail. I couldn't believe I knew more about what was in that letter than she did.

Brooke didn't even touch the envelope. It sat in the middle of the table, next to the salt and pepper shakers. I watched Brooke's face harden. Her smile faded, and her eyes got serious.

"Neat Guys, you can head up for dinner," Eddie announced. We were first in line for the second time that day. Lasagna and garlic bread. Yum.

"I hate lasagna!" Brooke said, and she started to cry.

Tammy bumped hips with her. "So don't eat. We'll fill up on candy and popcorn tonight." She squeezed her shoulder. "Come on, I'll get salad with you."

Brooke rested her head on Tammy's shoulder for a moment, and then they walked off to the salad bar together.

That was the Tammy I loved. But I'd be a liar if I said it didn't hurt to see her heap her tenderness on Brooke instead of me. Even though I knew Brooke needed it.

• • •

Working at canteen was as fun as I'd imagined it would be. Eddie trained us for fifteen minutes, and then before he opened the doors to all the campers, he told us we needed to be initiated. "Who wants to go first?"

Nobody volunteered, so Eddie picked Delaney. "Get over here, little Reed."

Delaney's eyes opened wide. We had no idea what this initiation would be. She walked over to Eddie, who was standing next to the Slushie machine. "Now, I want you girls to know there will be no horsing around in here." As he said this, he positioned a chair in front of the machine and sat Delaney down in it. "This is a serious business. A big responsibility." He tilted Delaney's head back, right under the spigot. He wouldn't do what I thought he was about to do. "I'm trusting you girls." Bam! He pulled the lever, and cherry Slushie squirted right into Delaney's mouth. We all squealed in delight. Delaney sat up laughing, red stains splashed on her cheeks. Eddie grinned from ear to ear. "Who's next?" he asked, and we all shouted, "Me!"

• • •

On Sunday, Darby woke us up early, and everyone was confused. "I've got your first clue!" she said. "We're going on our overnighter tomorrow!"

I jumped out of bed to see the clue. We all gathered around Darby and read:

Dear Cabin Six,
    We know you will have a **BALL** on your trip.
    The van is leaving tomorrow morning at eight-**THIRTY**.
    Don't make a **RACKET** as you look for clues!
    LOVE,
    Eddie and Maureen

"The tennis courts!" we shouted. We slipped into flip-flops and ran to the courts in our pajamas.

I didn't see any other clues at first, but then I spotted something orange taped to the fence. Looking closer, I saw it was an envelope with "Clue #2" written

143

on the outside. "Here it is!" I called, and everyone came over.

The next clue said:

Hey, Cabin Six,

You've gotten off to a nice st*ART*.

Such a bunch of **CRAFT**y girls!

On your trip you'll see **GREEN** mountains, **BLUE** waterfalls, and a **COLORFUL** sunset. We hope the **BROWN** porcupines will stay away!

Love,

Eddie and Maureen

"The arts and crafts building!" Annie said.
We found Clue #3 on the door:

Good job, Cabin Six!

You're getting close to your **GOAL**.

Don't forget to pack sleeping bags, bug spray, and flashlights that **SHIN**e.

Let's **KICK** it into gear, girls!

Love,

Eddie and Maureen

"The soccer field!"

We found the next clue taped to the goalpost.

Are you tired yet, Cabin Six? Ready to **KEEL** *over?*

We hope **KNOT.**

Tomorrow you lucky **MATES** *will* **HIKE OUT** *on beautiful trails along the coast of* **LAKE** *Superior.*

Love,

Eddie and Maureen

We ran down the hill and over to the boat shed, where we found a CD marked "LAST CLUE!!!"

"Who has a CD player?" I asked.

"The gym!" Kat and Annie said at the same time.

Laughing, we skipped and ran over to the gym, put the CD in the player, and pressed PLAY. We were breathless and excited, waiting for something. We didn't even know what. We heard a little static, and then a mellow voice began to sing.

"It's 'American Pie'!" Kat said. "I love that song!"

I did, too. We sat quietly, catching our breath, listening intently. Was Eddie going to cut in with some sort of clue? Was the song itself a clue? A minute into the song, the chorus started, and we put our arms around each other and sang along. The rhythm picked up, and soon we were swaying, dancing, and singing together.

I looked around at my cabinmates, all six of us in wrinkled pajamas, slept-on hair, and smiles as bright as the sunshine streaming in through the dusty windows of the gym. The song wrapped itself around us, making us one. This was it. This was what camp was all about.

Finally the song slowed down and came to an end, and we stood there in silence.

"What does it mean?" Delaney asked the question that was probably going through all of our minds.

"Maybe it doesn't mean anything," I said. "Maybe the song was there just to bring us together, to put us in the right mood."

"I think you're right," Kat said. "That seems like an Eddie sort of trick. But where are we going?"

We took another look at all of our clues, going over every word. Brooke said, "What's on the shore of Lake Superior, and has mountains, hiking, waterfalls, and porcupines?"

"Porcupines," Annie said. "That's kind of weird."

"And familiar!" Kat said. "Last year, one of the cabins went to—"

Kat and Annie both finished the sentence together. "The Porcupine Mountains!"

Kat snorted, and we all laughed. I'd never heard of the Porcupine Mountains, but they sounded fantastic. I couldn't wait!

That night at Fireside, when Dani named the new Fire-lighter, I actually hoped I wouldn't get it. I'd been so busy all day, first with the overnighter clues, then with packing for our trip, then with making a booth for Car-nival Day, today's all-camp activity, that I hadn't had time to think about the letter from Brooke's dad. But now I couldn't think about anything else. I was a letter thief. Being Firelighter would feel like a big fat lie.

Of course, I didn't have to worry. It went to Sami Betman, one of Madison's friends. I was awardless. Again.

•••

"Ugh! What is that smell?" I said as soon as I woke up Monday morning. Something sour and disgusting pene-trated the air, and I thought I was going to barf. Then I heard the unmistakable sound of someone else barfing, and I realized that's what the smell was.

"Oh gross!" Kat said. "I can't listen to that!"

"Me neither." I tumbled out of bed and escaped the cabin. It was chilly this morning, and my feet were freezing in the cold dewy grass, but at least the air was fresh out here. Kat and Annie joined me outside. They were smarter and put on shoes and jackets first. I hopped around and rubbed my arms to try to get warm. Delaney came out of the cabin next, and she handed me a jacket, which I put on and zipped up. "Who's sick?" I asked. It had to be Tammy, Brooke, or Darby.

Delaney shrugged. Then Darby stuck her head out of the cabin door. "Good morning, campers!" she said with an exaggerated smile. "Lovely day, isn't it?"

"Who's sick?" Annie asked.

"I'm afraid it's Brooke. Will you go get the nurse?"

• • •

While the nurse took care of Brooke, I hung out in the Lodge with Annie, Kat, and Delaney and waited for breakfast. "Poor Brooke," Kat said. "She's going to miss the Porcupine Mountains."

Annie asked, "Do you think Tammy is going to stay here with her?"

My breath caught in my throat. Would she? It kind of made sense, knowing what I knew about Brooke's situation at home. She'd want someone like Tammy with her if she was sick. And Tammy would offer, absolutely. But Tammy shouldn't have to miss out on the overnighter.

"Well, I'd stay with you if you got sick," Kat said.

"Aw, thanks!" Annie said, and she gave Kat's shoulder a squeeze.

"That's different," I said, trying to convince myself. "You guys are twins. They're just cousins."

"And best friends," Annie said.

"Not really," I said.

Nobody said anything after that. Annie looked at Kat in their ESP way of communicating. But you didn't have to be a twin to know what she was thinking—that I was being ridiculous. That Tammy and Brooke were best friends, and clearly I couldn't handle it.

Maybe they were right.

Finally Delaney broke the silence by saying, "My guess is Eddie won't let any of us stay behind with Brooke. They'll probably keep her in the infirmary so nobody else gets sick."

I hoped Delaney was right.

17

At eight-thirty, we loaded up the van, and Tammy was there. Just as Delaney had predicted, Brooke was stuck in the infirmary, and the nurse hadn't let Tammy stay with her. I felt bad for Brooke. I would hate to be sick at camp. But I had to admit I was excited to be going on the overnighter with Tammy. I realized there would still be five of us, but with Brooke temporarily out of the picture, things would be different. It would be Tammy and me, just like old times. I bet that by the end of our trip, everything would be normal between us.

The first good sign came when we all found seats in the van. Tammy slid in next to me as if it was the most natural thing in the world, and we sat together for the two-hour ride into Michigan's Upper Peninsula. Kat and Annie sat together, and Delaney sat alone. I didn't think she minded too much. I figured Delaney had a way of being alone without being lonely.

Maureen drove, and she told us stories from summers past. "Oh, you should have seen Darby when she was about your age. All spit and vinegar, that one." Darby shook her head and smiled, as if she was embarrassed. I couldn't picture Darby any way other than how she was right now, all sunshiny and cool. "She got into so much trouble her first summer, Eddie had to convince me to let her come back the next year."

"That's not true!" Darby said, with laughter in her voice. She turned around in her front row seat, faced us, and tapped her finger against the side of her head. "Maureen's losing her mind, girls. Don't pay any attention to her."

Maureen laughed loudly and hit the steering wheel. "Alrighty, then, I guess I won't tell the girls about your first trip to the Porcupine Mountains. You know I haven't forgotten that one." Darby and Maureen caught each other's eyes, and I saw Darby knew exactly what Maureen was talking about.

"Oh no," Darby said.

At the same time, we all shouted, "Tell us!"

Maureen just nodded and said, "I'll save this one for tonight around the campfire." Then she closed her mouth, but her lips curved up, as if she couldn't help but smile at the memory.

"Why don't we sing something?" Darby suggested, clearly wanting to change the subject.

So we sang "American Pie," but since we couldn't remember all the words, we made up some of our own, laughing all the way.

• • •

When we arrived, we unloaded the van at our site, a flat piece of dirt and grass surrounded by tall pine trees, and, in the distance, rolling green mountains. There was a fire circle and a picnic table, and that was about it. "Where's the bathroom?" Tammy asked.

Maureen pointed to the woods and smiled.

"Seriously?" Tammy scrunched her nose. "What if I have to go number two?"

Darby reached into one of the cartons of supplies and tossed Tammy a roll of toilet paper. "Then here you go, hon. Remember to bury it."

No way would I ever go number two in the woods!

"I was just asking." Tammy threw the toilet paper back to Darby. "I don't really have to go." She looked at me, and I knew what she was thinking . . . yuck!

We set up the tents—one for Maureen and Darby, and another for the rest of us—and we collected wood for the fire. Tammy and I sat next to each other at lunch. We walked next to each other on our hike to Lake of the Clouds. We helped each other climb the waterfall. It was as if Brooke didn't even exist, and I felt secure, really secure, for the first time this summer. I did notice that Delaney was quieter than normal, even for her. I probably should have made an effort to include her, but this was my one chance to be a two-some, not a threesome. It was too good to pass up.

Back at the campsite, in the late afternoon, Maureen said, "I need two girls to help me with our campfire stew, two to make the salad, and one to help Darby set the table and replenish our water supply. Have I got any volunteers, or do I need to enlist you?"

"We'll make stew!" Tammy said, holding my hand up in the air with hers.

"We'll do salad," Kat and Annie said at the same time.

Delaney didn't say anything at all. Darby put her arm around her and said, "I guess it's just you and me, kid."

Delaney blew out a breath. Her eyes were sad and maybe even a bit angry. I offered her a smile that she didn't return. I started to feel crummy for ignoring her all day.

Maureen said, "Okay, girls, let's get to work," and she motioned for Tammy and me to join her by the fire. Darby and Delaney went off to get water, and I told myself not to worry too much about Delaney. She'd understand. She knew how badly I wanted things to be better between Tammy and me.

"Campfire stew is one of my favorites, girls. Easy

and delicious. Tammy, you go ahead and chop up this onion, and, Jemma, you open up these cans of veggies." She handed me a can opener and two cans of generic mixed vegetables. Tammy started chopping the onion, and Maureen browned some ground beef in a big pot over the fire. The onion fumes and the smoke from the fire combined to make my eyes water, but it all smelled so good, especially mixed with the sizzling meat.

"How's that onion coming, hon?"

"Just about ready."

"Okay, then, we'll dump it in here soon as I drain the fat." Maureen poured off the grease into a can. Tammy added the onions, and I added the vegetables. "Ketchup!" Maureen said, as if she just remembered. "Jemma dear, go get a bottle of ketchup from the cooler."

I found the ketchup and squeezed the whole bottle into the pot. "Perfect!" Maureen said. "Now we just stir it every once in a while as it simmers." She inhaled deeply and smiled. "Nothing beats that smell, girls. Am I right?"

Quite honestly, the stew looked a little disgusting, but Maureen was right. It smelled tasty. "Do you make this every time you come here?" I asked.

"Mmm-hmm."

"Even on Darby's first trip here?" Tammy asked.

"Oh yes." It seemed Maureen was about to tell us the story when she stopped herself and smirked. "I see what you're doing." She wagged her finger at us. "Now, don't you try getting anything out of me just yet. That story's a doozy, and it needs to be told properly."

"Come on, Maureen. We'll act surprised when you tell us tonight!" Tammy said.

"Yes. Please?" I begged.

Maureen shook her head and laughed. But she didn't say another word.

Finally, with the stew thickened, the salad tossed, and the table set, we all wolfed down our dinner. Delaney was stuck eating peanut butter and jelly once again.

"When did you become a vegetarian?" I asked.

"I never liked meat, even when I was little. And when I was in kindergarten, I found out it actually came from animals. That freaked me out. It just seemed so cruel. And I haven't eaten meat since."

"Not even fish?" Tammy asked.

"Nothing with a mom."

When she put it that way, I felt a little bad. But still, I wasn't about to become a vegetarian.

"Do you ever miss it?" Kat asked. "I can't imagine life without hamburgers."

Delaney shrugged. "Not really."

Kat asked, "What if you had to eat a hamburger to save someone's life? Would you do it then?"

"Why would I ever have to eat a hamburger to save someone's life?"

"I don't know. Just answer the question."

"Okay, yes. I would. But I wouldn't like it."

"I once ate snails," Tammy said.

"Ew!" we all said.

"They were good. They're called escargots. They tasted kind of garlicky."

"I'm gonna barf!" Delaney said.

"We once ate shark," Kat said.

"In Aruba," Kat and Annie said together.

"It tasted like chicken," Annie said.

"I guess it's better than a shark eating you," I said, and everyone laughed.

Even Delaney seemed to be in a good mood. I was glad.

It was amazing how peaceful I felt without Brooke. I fantasized for a second that she'd be so sick she'd have to go home, but then I stopped. I didn't really want her to be sick. And truthfully, she didn't have a home to go to. Her dad was off with Jill somewhere. And her mom was apartment-hunting in Chicago.

After dinner we sat around the campfire and roasted marshmallows. I carefully kept mine away from the flame and rotated my stick as the marshmallow cooked. When it turned perfectly golden brown, I squished it between two graham crackers and a piece of chocolate to make a s'more. Mmmmm! There couldn't possibly be anything better than this.

We were all stuffed and sticky by the time Maureen

took her guitar out and began to play. The moon shone down on us, and the crickets added their music to Maureen's melodies. We sang "If I Had a Hammer," "You've Got a Friend," and a song in a Native American language. We repeated the foreign words after Maureen, the sounds seeming to gather power from the feel of the music. Kat got up and danced around the fire, and Annie beat out a rhythm on her lap. Ever since their big fight, I'd barely seen Annie dance at all, and Kat seemed okay with that. We applauded when the song ended. Then Maureen asked, "Any requests?"

"Yes," Tammy said. "Tell us the story about Darby."

Maureen strummed a chord on her guitar and shared a smile with Darby. "May I?"

"I don't think I have a choice," Darby said.

"Darby was ten years old that first summer, and, oh, was she a pistol," Maureen said. "Some girls get sad when they're homesick. Others get mad. That was our Darby. Mad as a hornet without a home. In all my years of camping, I've never seen a case of homesickness like our dear Darby Coleman's."

Darby put her hands over her face, looking embarrassed. I was intrigued. Darby? Homesick? It seemed impossible.

"Darby fought with each and every one of her cabinmates that summer. Just about every day, we heard another complaint about her. Eddie and I talked to her. We even let her call her parents. But she never stopped wanting to go home. I think she thought if she was terrible enough, we would *make* her go home, but that's just not our way, is it, Darby?"

Darby shook her head and grinned.

"So I took her cabin group here to the Porcupine Mountains, and Darby figured this was the perfect escape route for her."

"She ran away?" I asked, shocked.

"Mmm-hmm." Maureen nodded. "And not just once. She ran off twice. First, while we were on a hike, that very same trail we took you on today. That foolish girl got herself lost."

"Wait a minute," Darby said. "I wasn't lost. I was hiding. There's a difference."

"Not to us, there wasn't. We had to call the park ranger, and I nearly pulled all my hair out worrying about you. Then you walked right into the campsite as we were serving up dinner, as if nothing was wrong."

"Well, I'd gotten hungry, and who could resist that stew?" Darby had a sheepish look on her face. Maureen rolled her eyes.

"How did she run off the second time?" Kat asked.

"We were sitting around the campfire, telling ghost stories, and the next thing I knew, she was gone. I figured she was scared and had just gone inside the tent, but when the rest of the girls went inside to go to sleep, they said she was missing again. That was the last straw for me. A missing girl in the middle of the night in the

Porcupine Mountains! I swore when I found Darby she would get her wish. I would send that girl packing, no matter what Eddie said." Maureen shook her head, remembering. "Darby, hon, why don't you fill the girls in on your whereabouts that night?"

Darby's eyes twinkled. "Well, I was scared of the ghost stories. Especially one about a deranged killer here in these woods. And at first I did go into the tent. But I could still hear the girls telling this awful story about a man with a bloody hand, strangling children in the forest, so I hid again. This time in the camp's station wagon. I fell asleep in the backseat."

Maureen shook her head and looked to the sky. "She fell asleep in the backseat. And did she wake up when I got in the car and drove around the wilderness looking for her? No, she did not!"

"I was a sound sleeper. Plus, I was exhausted from all our hiking."

"You can't imagine the fright she gave us. And then, of course, when morning came, Darby stepped out of the car as if nothing was amiss. I nearly had a heart attack."

"So did you send her home?" Annie asked.

"Well, I tried. I told her she'd won. She could go home. Enough was enough. And, Darby, hon, tell them what you said."

Darby laughed. "I said I wanted to stay."

"After all that?" I asked.

"I can't explain it," she said. "I thought I wanted to go home. I thought if I was bad enough, they'd send me home. But as soon as I got my wish, I changed my mind. I realized I liked it here."

"You were a troublemaker," Tammy said, her eyes laughing.

"Yes, I was."

"But four years later, Darby was a Firelighter," Maureen said. "And now she's one of our best counselors. So it just goes to show you."

Maureen didn't say what, exactly, it went to show, but I thought about the story, and I decided she meant that people can change. And that at camp you'd always get a second chance. Or even a third. And I liked that. I did. With all the mistakes I'd made, I knew I'd need them.

I looked at Delaney and wondered how I'd make it up to her for spending the whole day with Tammy. I'd figure something out.

18

The next morning the birds woke me before the sun had a chance to peek over the mountains. My back was sore. We'd swept the dirt floor before putting up our tent, but, clearly, we hadn't done such a great job. I was pretty sure I'd slept on a few rocks. I rolled over in my sleeping bag and tucked my knees into my chest.

"G'morning," Delaney whispered to me. "Do you want to go for a walk?"

I knew I should go with Delaney, but I didn't want to leave Tammy. "Maybe later, okay?"

Delaney nodded and crawled out of her sleeping bag. She pulled on some shoes and a jacket and left the tent. I rolled back to face Tammy. She was asleep, her lips slightly parted, breathing deeply into her baby blanket, which was balled under her face. With Brooke gone, everything was perfect between us, just as I knew it would be. Maybe today we'd go back to camp and sign up for the Star Lake Cup.

A few minutes passed until Tammy stirred, wiped her eyes, and sat up. "Hey," she said.

"Hey."

She rubbed the back of her shoulder. "Oh man, I'm sore."

"Me too."

"And I've gotta pee. Come with me?"

"Sure."

We left the tent, breathing in the crisp, clean air, and we walked into the woods. Dried leaves and sticks crunched under our feet as we made our way to a spot we'd found yesterday. There was a skinny tree perfect for holding on to as we squatted backward and peed. I was in mid-stream when I heard footsteps coming toward us from deep in the woods. One look at Tammy's face, and I knew she heard them, too.

"Oh my God! I can't stop!" Tammy said, laughing.

"Me neither!"

"Who's there?" Tammy called out.

"Sh!" I said. "What if it's a deranged killer or something?"

That made Tammy convulse with laughter. Her face was red. I finished peeing and pulled my pants up as fast as I could. But Tammy couldn't do anything except shriek with her pants around her ankles. All of a sudden, I saw it was Delaney, and I cracked up. Tammy and I were both dying of laughter.

"She . . . thought . . . you were . . . a . . . killer!" Tammy said, barely able to spit the words out between giggles.

Delaney shrugged without smiling. "Sorry to disappoint you." Then she walked past us toward the campsite.

Guilt flooded my insides, drowning all my silliness. Tammy finally controlled her laughter and pulled up her pants. "No offense, Jem," she said. "I know you're friends with her, but she's weird."

I tensed. I wanted to say what Tammy wanted to hear, no matter what the truth was, because I wanted our friendship to be strong. But I couldn't. I liked Delaney. She'd been kinder to me all summer than everyone else in the cabin put together. And she wasn't afraid to be herself, even if that self was sometimes strange or different. "She's not so weird once you get to know her," I said.

Tammy raised one eyebrow at me as if I must have been kidding.

"Really," I said. "I'm not saying she could ever take your place, but—"

"Well, duh!" Tammy said with a smile.

I smiled back and tried to ignore the wobbly feeling in the pit of my stomach.

• • •

We got back to camp in the middle of lunch and went straight into the Lodge. I took a whiff and knew it was sloppy Joes, my favorite. "Yum," I said to Tammy. "I'm starved."

"Me too," she said. "But I'm going to check on Brooke first."

"Oh," I said, feeling the happiness from our overnighter melt away. "That's a good idea. Do you want me to come with you?"

"No, that's okay. I'll be right back."

I watched Tammy talk to Eddie, then leave the Lodge. I tried to hold on to that feeling of security I'd had on the trip, but it seemed like water running through my fingertips.

Cabin Woods started the "Announcements Song," and I joined in with the hope that singing would bring me to that carefree, confident place again. When the song ended, I felt a little better. Of course Tammy would check on Brooke. That was the nice thing to do. And Tammy was nice. That was one of the reasons I liked her.

Eddie took the microphone and said, "Good afternoon, campers! And welcome back, Cabin Six." He looked at a piece of paper and said, "Today at open period, tennis, sailing, swimming, riding, and crafts will be available. And Todd wants me to tell you there will be tubing at the ski dock." Everyone cheered. Tubing was the best. It was way easier than skiing. "Nancy wanted me to remind you that today is the last day to sign up for the Star Lake Cup. And tonight's evening program is—drum roll, please . . ." Everyone banged on their tables, creating a loud drumming sound. "Sheet sliding!"

A huge cheer went up in the Lodge. Kat and Annie gave each other high fives. I guessed sheet sliding must be awesome. But I was still focused on the Star Lake Cup. I had to talk to Tammy about it today.

Annie, Kat, Delaney, Darby, and I went up to the cafeteria line, and I helped myself to a big sloppy Joe sandwich and some Tater Tots. Delaney made a salad. On my way back to our table, Delaney called my name. Was she going to confront me about ignoring her? I knew I needed to apologize. I just hadn't done it yet.

"Hey," she said, looking at her salad. "Did you hear Eddie?"

"You mean about sheet sliding?"

"No." She licked her lips. "The Cup. Do you want to sign up with me?"

I shifted my weight from one foot to the other. I didn't know what to do. I liked sailing with Delaney, but my heart was still set on racing with Tammy. I had to believe that when it came right down to it, Tammy would sail with me. She'd pick me. And if she didn't, then . . . well, I wouldn't sail at all. There. I'd decided.

"I'm really sorry, Delaney, but I'm still planning to sail with Tammy."

"Oh." She stared at me, and I saw her disappointment even though she didn't say a word. I was the one who looked away first. I started to walk back to the table when I heard Delaney say, "Well, good luck, then."

I didn't know why her words made me feel so terrible, but they did. By the time I sat down, half the cabins were finished and clearing their places. I barely tasted my sloppy Joe.

"Uh-oh," Kat said, pointing with her eyes toward the counselors' table.

"What?" I asked.

"Darby and Todd. Look."

I didn't see what was wrong. "What? They aren't doing anything."

"Exactly. Todd didn't hug her hello and he didn't even save her a seat."

"Maybe he didn't want to hug her in the middle of the Lodge," I said. "And maybe he didn't know she'd be back in time for lunch."

Annie and Kat looked at each other knowingly. "There's trouble in paradise," they both said. But I was sure they were wrong. Darby and Todd were perfect together. One day we'd all be at their wedding.

We finished lunch before Tammy returned. I was so distracted by watching the door for her that I ended up losing Noses. Kat, Annie, and Delaney left the Lodge while I went up to get a sponge. Just as I finished wiping the table, Tammy walked in, and my spirits lifted. "Hi!" I said.

"Hi. Do you think there's any food left?"

"I don't know. Let's see." I walked with her over to the cafeteria line. The kitchen staff was putting everything away.

"Shoot," Tammy said.

"There's PB&J," I said, looking at the big tubs of peanut butter and jelly still sitting out.

"I guess."

I waited with her as she made a sandwich. "So how's Brooke?"

"Better. She hasn't thrown up today. The nurse said she can return to the cabin tomorrow."

"That's good." I followed Tammy back to our table and sat next to her. We were the only two people in the dining room. "Today is the last day to sign up for the Star Lake Cup," I said, deliberately cheerful and full of confidence. "So I thought I'd go down at rest hour and take care of it."

Tammy stopped chewing. She put her finger up as if to say "Hold on a second." Then she swallowed, looked at the table, and finally up at me. "Jemma, please don't make this into a bigger deal than it is, but I have to sail in the Cup with Brooke."

My heart squeezed tight. "But why?" My voice came out all squeaky.

Tammy shrugged. "I don't know. I just do."

I wondered if this was all because of Brooke's dad. Or was it more than that? Was this Tammy's way of telling me once and for all that she liked Brooke more than me? Either way, one thing was clear. Tammy had been stringing me along this whole time. "You were never going to sail with me, were you?" Stupid voice, cracking again.

"Jemma, don't get hysterical."

"I am not hysterical!"

"Then stop screeching."

"I am not screeching!" Maybe I was, but I didn't care. I pushed away from the table and stood, looking down at Tammy. "All summer long you've made excuses for Brooke. You put her first every chance you had— even when she was rude and mean to me. And you expected me to just take it. From Brooke. *And* from you."

Tammy shook her head. "I knew you were going to make a big deal out of this. That's one of the problems, don't you see?"

"No, I don't. I don't see anything except my best friend ditching me for her obnoxious cousin."

Tammy stood and faced me, nose to nose. "She's not obnoxious, Jemma. At least not to me. You're just jealous. And I can't deal with that anymore. You turned this summer into a gigantic tug-of-war, with me in the middle. How do you think that made *me* feel?"

"You?" I glared. She was complaining about her feelings when I was the one who'd been ditched? "You know what? I wouldn't sail with you if you were the last person on earth! Good luck in the race, Tammy Erikson. 'Cause you're gonna need it."

I stormed out of the Lodge, slamming the door behind me.

19

I ran, anger pulsing through my body. I needed to get away from Tammy, from everyone. I didn't know where I was running until I got to the gooney birds and stopped. I remembered arriving at camp, seeing this entrance for the first time. Even then I knew things weren't right with Tammy and me. I knew it, but I chose not to know it. Well, now there was no denying it. Tammy and Brooke were best friends, and I was out of the picture. I hated Tammy for hurting me, but in a weird way, it was a relief, this knowing. It was as if I'd been a juggler all summer long, keeping bowling balls and eggs and even knives up in the air, and finally they were all crashing to the ground.

I knew what I had to do. I needed to find Delaney, apologize, and ask her to sail with me in the Star Lake

Cup. Because I wanted to win that race, now more than ever. I wanted to beat Tammy and Brooke. And if I sailed with Delaney, we'd have a chance to make that happen. I just hoped Delaney would forgive me. After the way I'd treated her at the Porcupine Mountains, after I'd just told her I didn't want to be her partner for the Cup, I wasn't so sure about that at all.

• • •

When open period came, I found Delaney at the ranch. She looked up as I approached, then turned her back to me and focused her attention on the goat she was feeding out of her hand. This was not going to be easy.

I took a deep breath. "Hey," I said, "can I talk to you?"

She shrugged, but didn't turn around. I walked in front of her. She kept her eyes down. "Listen," I tried. "I messed up. A bunch."

Still nothing.

I got down on my knees. "I'm a complete idiot."

Delaney looked at me and smiled a tiny bit.

"Do you want to go sailing?" I asked.

She licked her lips as she considered.

"Please?"

Tossing the rest of the goat food on the grass, she wiped her hands and said, "Okay."

• • •

We were in the green boat, the one nobody wanted. And we were barely moving because the wind was so light. I knew I had to apologize. But I didn't know where to begin. Sorry for being nice to you only when Tammy wasn't being nice to me? Sorry for thinking you were weird? Sorry for not treating you like a real friend, when that's what you are? I finally said, "I'm sorry, Delaney. I shouldn't have ignored you like that on our overnighter. And I should have signed up for the Cup with you. You were right all along. I'm really, really sorry."

She stared straight at me in a way that made me feel as if she was looking deep into my soul. "I forgive you," she said.

Just like that.

My heart did a little flip-flop. And suddenly I had this urge to tell Delaney everything. I explained how lonely I was when Tammy moved away. How I believed so strongly that we were best friends *forever*, and nothing would ever change. But of course everything did change. I told her that I didn't put any effort into my other friendships in fifth grade because I thought I had Tammy. I told her about my countdown to camp and how I dreamed about sailing in the sunset boat with Tammy. I told her that for whatever reason, winning the Star Lake Cup with Tammy had gotten so twisted in my mind that I thought getting our names engraved on that trophy would make our friendship last forever.

Delaney listened and nodded and said, "Yeah, that makes sense," in all the right places. It felt so good to say all of this aloud and to have someone hear me and understand, that tears started flowing from my eyes. And there was absolutely no stopping them.

Finally Delaney said, "I think we better try to get back to camp."

I looked around and saw that we were near some summer homes, but camp was far behind us. There was still almost no wind. It wasn't going to be easy to sail back. I wiped my salty cheeks and said, "Uh-oh."

"That's okay," Delaney said. "Let's try to come about." She pushed the tiller toward the sail, but there wasn't enough power to complete the turn. We drifted closer and closer to someone's dock. There was a mom and dad, a dog, and a small boy playing in the water. The dad shouted, "Y'all need some help?"

"No, we're fine!" I called back. They looked innocent enough, but the truth was, they were strangers. We could end up on a milk carton if we weren't careful. "Let's jump in," I said to Delaney. "We can swim to camp."

"With the boat?"

"Of course. It's either that or wait for Nancy to rescue us." Nobody liked being rescued by Nancy. It was embarrassing.

"Okay."

We jumped in and turned our boat around. We hung

on to the stern and kicked, but the boat was really hard to control, so I grabbed the bow, and Delaney stayed in the back, and we made slow progress toward camp.

"I have to ask you something," I said. "And I hope you don't think this is too strange a question, but . . . why have you been so nice to me this summer?"

"Why wouldn't I be?"

"Well, I haven't treated you the way a friend should."

"I don't know about that. We had fun together at sailing and at the social. And lots of other times."

"That's true, but . . ."

"But what?"

"Never mind," I said. "We did have fun."

We didn't say anything for a while. It took a lot of energy to swim with the boat. As we got closer to camp, Delaney asked, "Do you really think we could win the Cup?"

I considered that we'd just learned to sail a few weeks ago, that we were smaller and younger and less experienced than most of the other girls who would be in the race. But then I thought about how badly I wanted it, and about the way Delaney focused when she practiced yoga. There was a strength and determination in her face that made me think she could do anything she set her mind to. "Yes," I said. "I do. You're a great sailor, and Madison is going to have to realize that. You deserve to shine, Delaney."

"We would both shine, wouldn't we?"

Beating Tammy and Brooke really would feel great. "We'll go down in camp history," I said. "Don't you think?"

"Sounds like a good plan to me," she said. "I love it! Woo-hoo!"

• • •

That evening, Eddie and Maureen rolled a huge plastic sheet over the hill, turned on a warm hose, and squeezed out a bottle of dish soap to make the biggest, sudsiest Slip 'n' Slide I'd ever seen. We were all in our swimsuits, waiting to take our turn to slide down the hill. Tammy and I were completely ignoring each other, when all of a sudden she called out, "Brooke!" and went running.

There was Brooke, in her little red bikini, running with her arms outstretched. They hugged and squealed as if they hadn't seen each other in years.

"What are you doing here?" Tammy asked.

"The nurse let me go."

"Yay!"

Kat and Annie hugged Brooke, too. Even Delaney acted happy to see her. I held our place in line, and when they all came over I said, "Glad you're feeling better," and I even gave her a hug. Then I listened as Brooke told about her stay in the infirmary. Yes, she was allowed to call her mom and watch movies on a little

TV. No, she didn't get to eat ice cream. It was almost our turn. Eddie was taking pictures while Maureen squeezed the soap bottle and Todd sprayed the hose. Brooke narrowed her eyes at Todd and shook her head. "Did you guys hear?" she whispered to us.

"What?" Tammy asked.

"They broke up!"

"No way!" Tammy said.

"I knew it!" Kat said.

It couldn't be true.

"What happened?" Kat asked.

"He's a cheater, that's what. I was lying in the infirmary, when Kelly and Morgan came in to get Tylenol, and I heard them talking. Todd went out with some girl from the Lake Gliders Ski Show while you were at the Porcupine Mountains."

"Poor Darby," Delaney said. "We should do something nice for her."

"Yeah," Kat agreed.

"I can't believe it," I said. "I thought they were going to get married."

"Married?" Tammy said, laughing. It was the first word she had spoken to me since the Lodge, and she was making fun of me. "Jemma, are you kidding? It was just a summer romance. They're like twenty years old."

My toes grabbed at the grass beneath me. "Well, I'm not saying it would happen today. I meant in the future. They're so cute together."

"*Were* so cute together," Brooke corrected. "Until Todd ruined everything. He's a total jerk. We should get him in trouble somehow."

"What do you mean?" Annie asked.

"I don't know. Maybe we can plant something in his room and say he stole our property. We could get him fired, we could make sure—"

"Your turn, girls," Maureen said. "Two at a time."

Tammy grabbed Brooke's hand and they went zooming down the hill. The four of us looked at each other in shock.

"Was she serious?" Kat asked.

"No way," Annie said. "That's crazy." They took their turn on the sheet slide.

But I had a feeling she was serious. And I bet it was all because of her dad. Poor Brooke. If she didn't read those letters and work things out with him, her problems were going to go from bad to worse.

"We're up," Delaney said, grabbing my hand. I pushed Brooke's problems out of my mind and took a running leap with Delaney onto the sheet slide. We flew down the hill, white, sudsy bubbles splashing into our faces as we laughed all the way.

20

The next morning at breakfast, Todd was wearing a surfer shirt, and his shaggy hair was damp from the shower, or maybe from an early morning ski session. He was shoving huge pieces of French toast into his mouth, not talking to anyone. Darby sat at the other end of the table, chatting quietly with some counselors. Thankfully, nobody had mentioned Brooke's crazy idea since yesterday, and I figured it was forgotten. But now Brooke said, "So what do you guys think? Should we do something mean to get back at Todd?"

An awkward silence hung in the air. Nobody wanted to go along with Brooke's plan, but we were all so used to doing whatever she wanted. I had to find a way to change the direction of the conversation. "Why don't we do something nice for Darby instead?" I suggested.

"Like what?" Brooke asked, scrunching her nose.

Delaney said, "Maybe we could make her bed for her."

"How is that going to help?" Brooke asked, scowling.

Delaney shrugged. "It's just something nice to do."

"We could make her a surprise party," I said. "We can decorate her room with hearts and love notes from us."

"Yeah," Delaney said. "Who needs Todd when she's got us?"

Kat beamed. "That's a great idea!" Brooke rolled her eyes, but everyone else agreed. Even Tammy.

• • •

That afternoon at sailing, Nancy looked at her clipboard and said, "Okay, girls, it looks like we have three pairs of sailors from this class entering the Star Lake Cup, Leah and Zoey, Tammy and Brooke, and Jemma and Delaney." I smiled at Delaney when she said our names. "Today you'll learn how a race starts." Nancy held up three colored flags, one blue, one yellow, and one red. "Can anyone tell me what these flags mean?"

"On your mark, get set, go?" Brooke asked.

"That's actually correct," Nancy said, smiling. "This yellow flag means you have five minutes until the race starts. The blue flag means two minutes. And the red flag means go. Why do you think we need these flags? Why don't we just shout 'On your mark, get set, go'?"

Delaney put her hand halfway in the air, and Nancy nodded in her direction. "Because the boats are moving at the start of the race. And you might not be able to hear."

"Good! Very good. You girls are smart, smart, smart!" Nancy drew three circles representing the triangle course on the whiteboard; then she drew a dotted line crossing the path between the first and third buoys. She made a small circle at one end of the line and a rectangle at the other. "This circle is a buoy. This rectangle is the pontoon boat. And this dotted line is where you'll start and finish the race. You can't actually see the line on the lake, but you'll have to imagine it's there. When the yellow flag is raised on the pontoon boat, you'll be tacking back and forth behind the line. When the blue flag comes up, you'll want to be ready. But don't cross the line yet, or else you'll have to circle back and lose precious time. And if you don't circle back, you'll be disqualified. When the red flag is raised, we'll sound the foghorn, and the race will begin.

"The main thing to remember is to stay behind the line before the race starts and to respect the right-of-way rules. There will be a lot of boats in a very small space. Every year we have a few crashes before the Cup even begins."

It all sounded so exciting. I couldn't wait.

"So," Nancy said, "we don't have much wind today, but you might as well get out there anyway. It's important to know how to sail in any kind of weather. We've only cancelled the race once in the history of the Cup. And that was because there was lightning and a tornado warning."

Delaney and I rigged the pink-and-green preppy sailboat, and we practiced the course as best we could with the little wind we had to work with. "I think I can swim faster than this," I told her as we tried to come about at the first buoy.

"Let's just hope the wind picks up by Friday," Delaney said.

"Yeah," I said, "or the race might not end until Saturday!"

• • •

That night, when Darby went to the shower house before the Talent Show, we moved into action. Kat and Annie had construction paper, markers, scissors, and tape. We all cut out hearts and decorated them. Tammy and I were still basically ignoring each other, so when she sat next to me and told me she thought this had been a really nice idea, I was caught off guard. "Thanks," I said. Was that her way of trying to make up with me? Was I supposed to just forgive and forget? She had hurt me too much for that. So I didn't say anything more. I went to the bathroom, and when I came back, I sat next to Delaney, as far away from Tammy as possible.

I wrote #1 COUNSELOR on one heart, WE LOVE YOU, DARBY on another, and DARBY + CABIN 6 = TRUE LOVE FOREVER on a third. Brooke made a huge one and wrote TODD STINKS on it. I thought that was mean. After all, the other day, Darby really liked Todd. Why would it be okay to insult him now? Just because they broke up didn't mean Darby's feelings had completely changed. Or had they? I had to admit, all this stuff confused me. Why was everything so temporary? Couldn't any relationship last forever?

Tammy laughed at Brooke's message, and they decided to tape that one up on the door to Darby's room so it would be the first thing she'd see.

When Darby returned, we lined up in front of her room. She was wearing a pink bathrobe and pink fuzzy slippers, and her hair was wrapped in a pink towel. "What's going on, girls?" she asked suspiciously.

"One, two, three," Kat counted, and we broke into the "We love you, Darby" song. Then we parted so she could see her door.

Darby took one look at the big TODD STINKS heart and laughed. Then she scolded us. "You guys are crazy and sweet, but that's not very nice." She took the heart off, opened the door, and gasped. Every surface of her room was covered with hearts and love notes from us.

"You guys!" Tears glistened in her eyes, but she had a huge smile on her face. "I can't believe you did this for me. Thank you. Oh, I'm gonna miss you girls. Come here." She spread her arms out, and we all snuggled around her for a big pink hug.

• • •

The Talent Show was starting in an hour. I wasn't worried about my gymnastics routine, but Kat and Annie were in a panic, trying to get all their costumes together. I didn't think they were going to do that Beyoncé dance, but they still had the dances from their classes—five of them! "Where's my black sparkly leotard?" Kat asked as she threw everything from her cubby into the middle of the cabin floor. Annie helped her pick through the mess, but the leotard was missing. "Does anyone have a black leotard I can borrow?" Kat asked. "I don't care if it's sparkly or not."

I had only brought one leotard to camp. It was blue, and I was wearing it. So there wasn't much I could do.

"I've got one in here somewhere," Brooke said. She dug through her cubby, reaching farther and farther back. She finally pulled it out, and as she did, five or six letters from her dad spilled to the floor. I nearly had a heart attack. Brooke looked around quickly to see if anyone had noticed the letters. We all had. Nobody said a word as she picked them up. My eyes were glued to those letters. Please, please, please, don't notice the one that's open, I prayed. Finally Brooke snapped, "What's everyone looking at?" So we turned away. I continued my silent plea as I pretended to be engrossed in a piece of lint on my bed. My heart was pounding so hard, I thought it might leap right out of my body.

All of a sudden, Brooke said, "Wait a minute!"

I froze.

"Who opened this?"

Slowly I looked up. Brooke was holding the envelope out as if it were a bloody knife found at the scene of a crime. Evidence. Her face was a mixture of shock and anger and maybe something else. Maybe fear.

The weight of what I'd done hit me like a boom to the head. I'd invaded her privacy. I'd hurt her. I'd crossed a line that never should have been crossed. Just like her dad had done. And I could pretend it hadn't been me, but that wouldn't take away any of Brooke's hurt. Or any of my guilt. I needed to confess. That was the right thing to do. But my mouth was wired shut.

Brooke glared at each of us, one by one, accusing. I noticed tears in the corners of her eyes. "Somebody opened my mail," she said.

Now was my chance. Come on, Jemma, say something! But I sat there, silent.

Brooke said, "God! Can't a girl have any privacy at this camp?" And she stormed out of the cabin, letters in hand.

We all looked at each other, not knowing what to say. Finally Tammy said, "Those letters are from her dad."

"Really?" Kat asked. "Why won't she read them?"

"She's mad at him, and well . . . it's complicated," Tammy said. "I don't think she'd want me to talk about it, anyway."

"Wow, I can't imagine being so mad at someone that I wouldn't even read their letters," Annie said. "What if he's writing to apologize?"

"Maybe Brooke isn't ready to forgive," I said, suddenly realizing that was exactly it. "So if she doesn't open the letters, she doesn't have to deal with that."

Tammy looked at me, surprised. I was surprised, too. I was seeing things through Brooke's eyes. And the weird part was, they didn't feel that different from my own.

• • •

Brooke came into the gym halfway through the Talent Show. I could tell she'd been crying. Her eyes were swollen, and her nose was pink. I wondered if she'd finally read the letters. Or had she ripped them into tiny pieces and thrown them in the trash? I hoped not.

The Talent Show rocked, and my gymnastics routine was fun. After all the classes had done their acts, Eddie introduced the final number of the night, the Outrageous O'Reilly Sisters. I was surprised Annie had decided to perform with Kat, after all. They walked out on the stage wearing black leotards and purple wraps. But instead of the two of them dancing to that Beyoncé song, Kat danced a solo while Annie played her bongos.

They were amazing, and everyone gave them a standing ovation. I thought about how they had a forever relationship. It wasn't a summer romance. It wasn't a friendship that could wither and die. It wasn't a marriage that could end in divorce. Even if they fought, they'd be sisters forever. I didn't have a twin sister, but I did have Mom, Dad, and Derek.

After the show, I hugged Kat and Annie and said, "You were awesome."

"Thanks," they both said at the same time. Kat snorted, and we all laughed.

21

That night, as I was changing for bed—without caring about anyone seeing me—Darby came into the cabin and said, "After everyone's washed up, we're having a cabin meeting. Okay?"

I swallowed hard and looked around at my cabin-mates. Nobody said a word. We all knew what this was about. I tried to breathe normally, but I felt as if I were underwater. I put on my pajamas, brushed my teeth, and did my best to appear innocent. I thought I was going to throw up.

We sat in a circle on the floor of the cabin. The only light came from the bathroom and the moon outside. Darby was sitting next to Brooke. "So," Darby said, "I understand that someone invaded Brooke's privacy, and I think we need to talk about that."

Nobody said anything.

"This cabin is like a family," Darby said. "This is your home away from home. These are your sisters. We need to be able to trust each other, right?"

I nodded along with everyone else.

"I think whoever opened Brooke's mail probably feels terrible right about now." Darby looked at each of us. When her eyes got to mine, I thought I would die right there on the spot. But I didn't. I hung around for more torture. "There are only two more days of camp, and I know you're not going to want to go home holding these terrible feelings inside of you for the whole school year. So I hope whoever did this will find the courage to apologize to Brooke. Okay?"

Still nobody spoke.

Darby sighed. "Look, we all make mistakes. You guys heard about a bunch of mine at the overnighter, right?" She smiled, and a little of the tension was let out of the room. "But that's how you grow. You make mistakes. You own up to them. You make amends. And you move on. A little wiser, hopefully." She squeezed Brooke's shoulder. "Two days," she repeated. And then she said good night.

I didn't look at anyone. I just got into bed, faced the wall, and pressed Henry against my eyes. He soaked up every last one of my silent tears.

• • •

I woke up Thursday morning feeling as though I'd had a gazillion dreams that I couldn't remember, but that left me completely restless. I had to confess to Brooke. But I'd have to do it when nobody else was around. Right after skiing, when we'd both be changing in the cabin, would be the perfect time.

It was the last day of regular activities and my last chance to get up on those big old skis and make it all the way around the lake. I didn't know why it was so hard for me. Knees bent. Arms straight. Lean back. Let the boat pull me up. I got it. But for some reason, my body still didn't.

"Today's your day!" Darby said to me from the boat, and she tossed me the towrope. I noticed that Darby leaned away from Todd in the boat, but that didn't stop her from being her regular bubbly self. Todd winked at me. Oh God, it made no sense, but I still had a ridiculous crush on him, even though he'd broken Darby's heart. I'd love to get up today. Maybe Todd would hug me, or at least give me a high five and one of his magnificently crooked smiles. Okay, today was my day. I was going to do it.

Todd pulled the boat slowly away from me, and I let the towrope slide through my fingers. Three big knots signaled that the tow bar at the end of the rope was coming, and I grabbed on to it tightly. There had been days when I missed the tow bar completely and Todd had to circle around again. But this time I grabbed ahold of it, and I was not letting go. I made sure the rope was between my skis. I was in the perfect tucked position.

"Hit it!" I shouted, and Todd revved the engine.

I was not going to let go of that towrope, no matter what. I let the boat pull me in the tucked position. Then, slowly, I rose, leaning back, arms straight. I was doing it! I was up! Waterskiing! Darby cheered for me in the boat. I looked down at my skis, skimming across the water. So cool!

Then, suddenly, I was off balance. I pulled the towrope toward me, which I knew I wasn't supposed to do. I tried to straighten my arms again, but there was slack in the rope, and fast as you could say "champion skier," I was in the water, face first, being pulled like a giant fish caught on a line. Water rushed into my mouth. This was it, I was going to drown. Everything moved in slow motion, yet it was all happening so fast. I didn't understand how to stop the water from pouring into my mouth. Then I heard Darby yell, "Let go!" And I realized I just had to close my mouth and let go of the tow bar.

So that's what I did. It was so simple that I started to laugh and cough and laugh some more. Todd circled the boat around, and Darby said, "Jemma, you've got to let go when you fall, sweetie!"

And I said, "Yeah, I think I've learned that one the hard way."

"Do you want another go?" Todd asked. "You almost had it. You just shouldn't have looked down."

"Definitely."

This time I got to standing again, and I kept my head up, my eyes on the green blur of trees along the shoreline. As the boat started its turn back toward camp, Darby signaled that I was about to hit some choppy water. I bent my knees extra low and squeezed the tow bar tightly as I rode over the waves. I was not going to fall. I was not going to fall. Tips up, head up, back and arms straight. And then, there was camp and the ski dock. I did it! I made it around the lake! The boat slowed down, and I let go of the tow bar and gracefully sank into the shallow water. Everyone in class stood on the dock and cheered. For me.

Everyone but Brooke. She wasn't there.

• • •

Brooke must have left class right after her turn, because she wasn't in the cabin when I went back to change. I had to admit, I was relieved. I was so proud of myself for skiing around the lake, I didn't want to ruin the moment by dealing with what I'd done to Brooke. There'd be time for that later.

During open period, Delaney and I practiced for the Star Lake Cup. The race was the next day, and this was our last chance to test the course. Nancy had brought in extra boats because there were twelve pairs of girls signed up. Delaney and I tried to grab the sunset sail, but Madison and Lisa beat us to it. Madison told Delaney, "Sorry, sis, but this is the sail we won with last year. It practically has our names on it."

I pretended the yellow sail was the one we wanted in the first place. Lisa said, "It's so cute that you guys entered the race! Isn't that cute, Mad? Little sixth graders trying to win the Cup!"

Madison tugged on Delaney's ponytail and smiled. "It is cute. Good luck, Laney."

Clearly, they thought we had no chance.

All twenty-four of us were out on the lake. As we tacked to the first buoy, with Madison and Lisa in front of us, I said, "Let's show them what you've got."

"What do you mean?"

"I mean, let's take the inside turn here. Let's cut them off just a little bit."

Delaney smiled mischievously. "You think we can?"

I shrugged. "We can try."

"I don't know. It seems like that's inviting bad karma into our lives."

"Oh, come on! This is a race. You know, with winners and losers? We have to do our best. And they are taking a very wide turn around the buoy. We'd really be helping them. Because if they see that we're able to cut them off today, then tomorrow, in the real thing, they'll take a better line around the buoy. So I think we're inviting good karma in."

Delaney squinted at me. "I'm not so sure, but okay. Ready about?"

"Hard alee!"

Delaney pushed the tiller toward the sail, and I pulled the mainsheet in as we turned super-close to the buoy. Madison and Lisa's boat came at the buoy from our right, and they jagged around us to keep from crashing.

"Hey! Watch out!" Lisa yelled.

"Right-of-way!" Madison called.

"Shoot! Shoot! Shoot!" Delaney said, shaking her head. "That was bad."

"It's okay. We're okay," I said. "We had the right-of-way!" I yelled back at them.

"Actually, I think they did," Delaney said.

"Really?"

Delaney nodded.

"Oops. Okay, so maybe that wasn't the best idea."

"Maybe not," Delaney said. "But we are ahead of them."

"Yes, we are!" I adjusted the sail and smiled. I had to admit, it was scary sailing so close to so many other boats, but it was exhilarating, too.

Tammy and Brooke sailed past us in the pink-and-purple girlie sail. Delaney looked at them, then asked me, "Who do you think read her letter?"

I looked at the sail. "I have no idea. Maybe nobody did. Maybe her dad just didn't seal the letter all the way.

You never know. I mean, why would anyone want to read her mail?"

Delaney said, "I don't know, but I was kind of curious about those letters. Weren't you?"

I shrugged.

"I mean, I'm not saying anyone should read another person's private stuff, but Brooke has been obnoxious all summer, and Darby never said a word about it. Now, all of a sudden, she gives us this big cabin talk and tells us we need to apologize to Brooke?"

Delaney was right. It didn't seem very fair. On the other hand, Brooke was going through something harder than I could ever imagine. But did that make it okay for her to be so mean? And did that make it okay for me to read her mail? No and no.

"It was me!" I blurted. "I'm the one who read her letter."

Delaney nodded. I had the feeling she'd already known.

22

I woke up Friday morning to the sound of the wind rattling our window. I poked my head out from under my blanket and saw my breath mist into a shivering cloud. The sun that normally poured into our cabin couldn't get through the overcast sky. What an ugly start to the last day of camp.

I pulled on my Star Lake sweatshirt, and put the hood up on my way to breakfast. Still the wind blew right through me. "Do you think they'll cancel the race?" I asked Delaney.

"I doubt it. Remember what Nancy said? They almost never cancel it." She shivered. "Maybe the weather will change."

I searched for even the tiniest patch of blue, but all I saw was different shades of gray.

We drank hot chocolate with mini-marshmallows as a special treat for breakfast. I looked out the window at Star Lake. Its surface was almost as rough as it had been on the night of the flying canoe. Everyone was talking about the weather. And everyone was bummed out. Finally Eddie came in to make the morning announcements. "Gooood morning, Star Lake girls!"

"Gooood morning, Eddie," we all shouted.

"Beautiful day today, huh?" Everyone groaned. "Unfortunately, this weather system looks like it will be with us all day, so we're going to have to make the best of the situation. The sailing race, tennis tournament, and riding show will go on as scheduled, unless it rains."

Someone from Cabin Woods shouted, "Or snows!" And everyone laughed.

"So make sure you show up for the event you chose. Let's bundle up and pull it together. You're the girls of Camp Star Lake. A little bad weather can't slow you down!"

Cabin Woods stood on their chairs and clapped the opening to our camp song. Then we all got up and joined them, drowning out the whistling wind.

After cabin cleanup, Kat and Annie played Spit. Since they weren't in the riding show, the tennis tournament, or the Cup, and it was too cold to come out and cheer for us, they'd decided to have a Spit marathon. Delaney practiced yoga. I knew enough not to expect her to skip her morning yoga routine. But still I wished she'd hurry up. I wanted to get to the sailing dock to make sure we lucked out with a good sail.

Tammy, Brooke, and I bundled up for the race. I put on a swimsuit, pajama pants, sweatpants, T-shirt, long-sleeve shirt, and sweatshirt. I wished I had a ski hat, but that was definitely not on the camp packing list.

Tammy and Brooke wore just as many layers. They left while Delaney was still doing a headstand with her legs balanced against our bunk bed, her YOGA GIRL shirt sliding up her belly. "Ready?" I asked hopefully.

Delaney didn't respond. Her face turned red from being upside down too long. It was useless to try to rush her. But I had so much nervous energy that I rocked from heels to toes and back again. Finally Delaney came down from her headstand and said, "Jemma, I know you think this is stupid, but just sit with me and meditate for five minutes."

Me? Meditate? With Kat and Annie right there to witness it? It was one thing to do a few Sun Salutations, but meditation was a whole other story. "All the good sails will be taken. We have to go."

"Well, I'm going to take five minutes, so you might as well join me. Let's center ourselves before the race."

"I could go down and get a boat, and you can meet me there."

"We're partners, right? We should stick together. Just do this with me, and if you hate it, I won't ask you to ever try it again. Okay?"

I sighed. "Fine. But I'm not saying 'Om.' "

Delaney smiled. "Of course not."

"Hey," Annie said. "We're going to do it with you, too. Come on, Kat, let's try it."

Kat shrugged and said, "Why not?" They put their cards down and joined us.

I sat cross-legged next to Delaney on her yoga mat. Kat and Annie sat on towels. Delaney showed us how to hold our hands in our laps with our thumbs touching. "Now just rest your eyes and your facial muscles," Delaney said in a calming voice. "Empty your mind and focus on your breathing."

There was no way to empty my mind. It raced ahead to the Cup. I hoped we didn't get stuck with one of the green or yellow sails. I hoped we finished in first place. Second place would be awful. So close but so far.

"Breathe in and out . . ."

If we didn't win, I hoped we'd at least beat Tammy and Brooke and Madison and Lisa. It would be the worst to lose to them.

"Inhale positive energy, and exhale all negative thoughts."

I breathed deeply and thought of winning, of doing our very best, of conquering that jibe turn. As I exhaled, I tried to force all my worries out of my body, but the only thing that left me was a stream of air. My mind was still running a million miles an hour.

"Breathe in confidence. Breathe out fear."

I peeked at Kat and Annie. They seemed to be totally relaxed. Why wasn't I?

"In and out. In and out."

How much more of this was I supposed to take?

"Ready?" Delaney asked quietly.

Not if ready meant calm, centered, and relaxed, I thought. But there was no reason to let Delaney know that meditating hadn't worked for me. That might delay us even more. Besides, I was ready in my own way. So I smiled and said, "Let's go!"

• • •

"I don't want any squabbling," Nancy said before holding out a hat with folded-up pieces of paper in it. Twenty of us stood in the boat shed (two pairs had dropped out of the race that morning), and Nancy was having us draw for sails.

"You do it," I told Delaney. I didn't want to be responsible if I picked a bad sail.

Delaney closed her eyes and chose a piece of paper. She unfolded it, and I saw it said GREEN. Ugh. But I told Delaney it was okay, it was just a color. Brooke and Tammy lucked out and got the shadow sail, my second favorite. Madison and Lisa would be in cotton candy. Nobody drew the sunset sail, and I asked Nancy if we could switch, but she said no trading.

My pants were rolled all the way up to my thighs as I waded out to the green boat. The nice thing about the air being so cold was that the water actually felt warm. But it was so choppy that the waves splashed up and got my pants wet. Not a good feeling!

Our boat rocked like crazy in the whitecaps as we rigged it. But we finally hoisted the sail, unhooked the boat from the anchor, and sailed from shore. I felt a little sick to my stomach, not from the motion, but from fear. Our sail was taut, and as the boat flew through the water, waves splashed up at us from every direction. My glasses were so wet they were useless. I finally took them off and stuck them deep in my pocket. I held on to the mainsheet for my life. "How are we going to do this?" I shouted to Delaney above the roar of the wind.

"I have no idea! We're just going to," she shouted back, spitting water that had flown into her mouth. Nancy was in the silver safety boat, putt-putting around the course. I felt a little better knowing she was there to rescue us just in case anything happened.

I was most worried about the start. All those boats zooming back and forth in the same space. It would be a miracle if we didn't crash. The yellow flag flew, and the other nine boats tacked near the starting line. We were behind them all, which I liked because it seemed safer, but which couldn't possibly be the way to win the race. "We have to move up," I told Delaney.

"Everyone's going so fast. I'm scared we'll crash."

The blue flag was raised. Two minutes.

"We have to! We'll never catch up otherwise."

Delaney licked her lips and steered us toward the rest of the boats. It was chaos. Boats flew up and down the line, zigging and zagging away from each other at the last second to avoid colliding. I held my breath and prayed we'd be pointed in the right direction when the foghorn blew. Every time we came about, the sail swung so strongly to the other side of the boat that it felt more like a jibe turn. My hands were wet and slippery, and I dug my nails into my palms as I gripped the sheet. If I let go, we'd be goners.

Red flag. Foghorn. Go!

Oh my God! It was a terrible start! There were six boats in front of us, including Madison and Lisa's and Tammy and Brooke's. And I thought I heard a whistle right after the foghorn blew. "What's that whistle?" I asked Delaney.

"I don't know. But I think it means someone crossed the line before the start. It might have been Madison and Lisa. They were first."

We headed out on a port tack. "So they have to circle back, right? Or else they'll be disqualified."

"Yes. If that's what that whistle meant. I don't know, Jemma. We have to focus."

So I focused. But I noticed that Madison and Lisa were not circling back.

The preppy boat passed us and sailed dangerously close to Madison and Lisa's. Tammy and Brooke were way out to the right. It was hard to tell if they were ahead of us or not. The first leg of the race involved the most decision making: how many times to come about, at what angle to approach the buoy . . . But Delaney didn't make any decisions. She just followed Madison, turning whenever she turned. With every tack, we fell a little farther behind.

"You can't keep following Madison!" I yelled to Delaney. "We'll never catch up."

"But she knows what she's doing."

"Well, so do you!"

Delaney pushed the tiller to the side. I pulled the mainsheet in, and we ducked. The wind gusted and blew our boat ahead. I swore we went airborne for a second, and my stomach lurched. I remembered what the wind had done to the canoe.

Up ahead at the buoy, two boats collided, and Nancy arrived in the safety boat to help them. There was such a crowd at the buoy, we had no choice but to make the world's widest turn. We were so far away, we were practically off the course. This was not looking good. But then, as we came past the buoy, it seemed as if we were in first place. That couldn't be right. I looked behind us and saw what happened. The cotton-candy boat and the yellow boat were trying to circle back around the first buoy. They must have missed the turn. Tammy and Brooke were catching up to us. This leg of the race was easier, just a straight reach. I trimmed the sail, and we hiked out. We were going so fast. Too fast!

The jibe turn was coming up, and I was terrified. We absolutely, positively, could not capsize.

"Ohmygod, ohmygod, ohmygod!" I said as we got closer to the buoy.

"Jibe ho!" Delaney yelled.

The force of the wind ripped the sheet right out of my hands. The sail flew. The boat tipped. And before I knew what was happening, I was floating in Star Lake, coughing up mouthfuls of water. So was Delaney. "Are you okay?" I asked her.

"Yes! Come on!" She started swimming around to the other side of the boat, and I followed. I didn't know what her rush was. There was no way we could win now. All my extra layers slowed me down, and the boat tipped higher and higher. The choppy waves pushed the mast down and the bottom of the boat up. We grabbed on to the centerboard, but the boat didn't tip back up. We both hung onto the board and caught our breath.

I watched Tammy and Brooke approach the jibe turn. They were going to win the race. And that was the worst. The absolute worst. But no! They capsized, too. My heart pounded. Two of the boats were still hung up at the first buoy, and the other six boats were on the second leg. If we got our boat up before Tammy and Brooke did, we might actually win. Yes!

Delaney pulled herself all the way up onto the centerboard until she stood on top of it. I was afraid it would break in half, but it didn't, and slowly the boat righted itself. We climbed in, and I grabbed ahold of the main-sheet. I took one last look at our competition. Madison and Lisa were coming up to the jibe turn. And behind them were two more boats, gaining ground. Tammy and Brooke's boat was still down. It didn't even look as if they were trying to get it up. Something was wrong.

"Pull the sail in!" Delaney shouted. "Come on!"

I squinted to see better. Tammy and Brooke were bobbing in the water, holding each other. "They need help," I told Delaney.

She looked at Tammy and Brooke. "I think you're right." We both peered toward the first buoy, where Nancy was still assisting the girls who'd crashed over there. "What should we do?"

Madison and Lisa executed a perfect jibe turn. Delaney blinked and wiped her eyes. If we stopped to help Tammy and Brooke, Madison and Lisa would win the race. Unless they had already been disqualified, and I couldn't be sure about that. But something told me Tammy and Brooke were really in trouble. Why else would they be holding each other like that?

I thought of our names on that trophy. I thought of Delaney finally getting the chance to shine, finally stepping out from her sister's shadow. And I thought of me beating Tammy and Brooke. Showing them . . . what? That I was better than they were? That Tammy had chosen the wrong girl? Right now it all seemed so fool-ish.

I knew what I had to do.

I handed the mainsheet to Delaney. "I'm going to swim over and help them," I said. "And you're going to finish the race."

"What? That's crazy! We can't split up."

"Come on, Delaney. This is your chance. Can you handle the boat on your own?"

"I think so, but I can't leave you out here."

"I'm a good swimmer. And it's not that far. And I have a life jacket. Please. Go. Win the race and show Madison what you're made of."

"No." She pushed the sheet back at me, but I didn't take it. "I'll stay with you, and we'll sail over together to help Tammy and Brooke."

"Delaney, please let me do this for you. You've done so much for me."

She looked at Madison and Lisa, speeding up to us, and I saw something change in her face. I knew I'd convinced her.

"Good luck!" I said and jumped into Star Lake. The waves crashed over my head, and I made slow progress with all my heavy clothes, but eventually I got to Tammy and Brooke and saw that Brooke's head was bleeding from a nasty gash at the top of her forehead.

"She got whacked with the boom," Tammy said with tears in her eyes.

Their boat was almost completely upside down, and I knew the first thing I had to do was get it up before it turtled and the centerboard floated away. I pulled myself up on top of the board, the way Delaney had on ours, and slowly the boat righted itself. Then I climbed in and straightened out all the ropes. "Brooke, do you think you can pull yourself up?"

"I don't know."

Just then I heard Nancy approach in the safety boat. She helped Brooke into her boat and asked Tammy and me if we could finish the race together. "Can't I come with you and Brooke?" Tammy asked, shivering in the water. "I'm freezing and freaked out and—"

But I interrupted her. "Tammy, let's finish the race together."

Nancy smiled and said, "I think you should. Brooke will be fine. I've got a first-aid kit right here. Go and finish the race. You're almost there."

I reached out to help Tammy into the boat. She took a deep breath, looked at me with a fair amount of doubt, then finally grabbed my hand.

23

So there I was sailing with Tammy in the Star Lake Cup, though the scene wasn't quite how I'd imagined it would be. Tammy pointed us toward the finish line, and I adjusted the sail. I had no idea if Delaney had won the race or not. She, Madison, and Lisa were all heading in toward camp already. I felt like one of those marathon runners you see on the news, finishing the race hours behind everyone else, thrilled just to get to the end.

We charged across the lake, my hands cold and cramped from holding so tight to the mainsheet, my whole body too tired to even try to talk to Tammy. As we sailed across the finish line, I saw a counselor on the pontoon boat mark down our time on her clipboard. That was it. The race was over. I looked at Tammy and shrugged. She shrugged back. And suddenly I realized I wasn't angry with her anymore. She'd moved, and then she'd moved on. She hadn't really been my best friend since fourth grade.

After we came about and started sailing back to the shore, Tammy seemed to realize what I'd done. "Wait a minute," she said. "You quit the race to help us."

I hadn't thought of it that way. "It didn't feel like quitting. It felt like doing the right thing."

"But still, Jemma, you would have won the race."

"Maybe. But Madison and Lisa probably did."

Tammy shook her head. "No way. They disqualified. I saw the counselor point to their boat when she blew the whistle at the start."

"Really?" That meant Delaney had won! How awesome! A wave crashed over the boat and splashed me in the face, but nothing could dampen my spirits now.

"That was cool of you, Jem." Tammy tugged on her earlobe.

I smiled. The truth was, I didn't need Tammy's approval. Under my wet layers of clothes, I felt a warm glow inside of me, deep inside. I felt better than cool. I felt like the camper I wanted to be—a camper extraordinaire.

• • •

Back in the cabin, Kat and Annie were still playing Spit. Delaney was combing tangles out of her hair. I congratulated her and gave her a huge hug.

"Ah! You're freezing!" she said. She had already changed into dry clothes, and I was still soaking wet.

"Sorry."

"That's okay. Can you believe it?" Her face was shining with joy.

"So it's true! You won!"

"*We* won. I couldn't have done it without you, Jem."

"But you're the one who crossed the finish line. The youngest camper ever to win the Star Lake Cup. You're amazing."

"That's what we were telling her," Kat said.

"What did Madison say?" I asked.

"It was funny." Delaney sat on my bed and hugged her knees to her chest. I started peeling off my wet clothes. "Lisa was saying that I should have been disqualified because there's a rule about having to finish a race with the same people you start with."

"Really? There is?"

"According to official sailing rules, yes. But Nancy said that particular rule wasn't something she had ever taught us, and it wasn't in keeping with the spirit and character of Camp Star Lake. Then Lisa cried and swore that they'd had a clean start, but Madison told Lisa to shut up! She said I'd won fair and square and that she was really proud of me."

"That's awesome!" I knew how fantastic that must have made Delaney feel.

I wished I could have taken a long, hot shower to

warm up after the race, but there was no such thing at camp. It was more like a warm trickle. I had to admit, I was the tiniest bit excited to go home and wash off a month's worth of dirt and lake water and sweat and bug spray, which seemed to have seeped into all my pores. But mostly I was sad that the summer was coming to a close. It had gone too fast and was ending too soon.

After my shower, I pulled on dry, comfy sweats and headed over to the infirmary. I'd put off apologizing to Brooke, and even if I couldn't get her alone, I knew I just had to do it.

She was sitting on the bed holding an ice pack to her head when I walked in. Tammy was next to her, wrapped in a blanket, and the nurse sat at her desk doing a crossword puzzle.

"Hey," I said, "how's your head?"

Brooke took the ice pack off to show me a swollen bump and a jagged cut. "At least I don't need stitches."

"But she might have a concussion. She's here for observation," Tammy said, making finger quotes around the words "for observation." The three of us looked at the nurse, who was so intent on her crossword puzzle, it didn't seem as though she would notice anything else.

"I am never sailing again!" Brooke said.

"Never?" I asked.

Tammy said, "Well, at least not in weather like that, right?"

"Yeah," Brooke said. "We almost drowned out there!"

I could have reminded her that we were all wearing life jackets, but I didn't want to argue. I'd come to apologize, and I knew I had to do it now, even with Tammy right there. So I took a deep breath and quietly said, "Brooke, I'm the one who read your dad's letter."

Tammy's eyes opened wide. Brooke's eyes narrowed. "I knew it was you," she said.

My breathing started to come fast. I wanted to run. I wanted to cry. "I'm sorry. I'm really, truly sorry."

Brooke didn't say anything. She just shook her head and turned away from me. Tammy mouthed the word "Why?" to me.

I looked deep into Tammy's light brown eyes. Didn't she know why? Didn't she get it? Tammy blinked, and I saw that her eyes were wet and that maybe, just maybe, they held a little understanding and forgiveness.

• • •

Brooke came back to the cabin in the late afternoon, as soon as the nurse decided she was concussion-free. It was pouring outside, and we were packing our duffels. I was sure I was going home with some of my cabinmates' things, and I knew I didn't have all of my stuff, but it didn't really matter. Besides, it would give us all an excuse to get together during the school year.

Just before dinner, Brooke asked if she could talk to me alone. Kat and Annie looked up from their duffels, and I knew in that moment they'd figured out I was the letter thief. At least there were no more secrets now. I took a deep breath, then followed Brooke into the bathroom.

"Why'd you do it?" she asked, leaning against the sink.

I had asked myself that question about a gazillion times already, and every time I came up with a different answer. Part of me was just plain curious. Another part (I'm ashamed to admit) was so angry at Brooke I didn't care about her privacy or her rights. And another part truly wanted to understand Brooke, to figure out why she had been so mean to me. "I don't know exactly. I guess I really wanted to make sense of you, to know why you acted the way you did."

"So you thought reading my private mail was a way to do that?"

"Look, it was wrong. The truth is, I was jealous of you, which doesn't excuse anything, I know."

A silent pause hung in the air. Then Brooke nodded. "Well, at least I know the truth."

She started to leave the bathroom, but I caught her arm. "Wait," I said. "One more thing. I want you to know I'm sorry about your dad. That must be really hard to deal with."

"It is."

I stood there for a second, thinking. I had hoped apologizing would wipe the slate clean, but I still felt kind of crummy about what I'd done and about everything that had happened with Tammy, Brooke, and me this summer. Maybe in time they would forgive and forget. And maybe I would, too.

• • •

The storm washed away the clouds, and the evening was damp and clear. After an amazing dinner of steak, rolls with butter, three kinds of salad, and two kinds of cake, the bell rang for one final friendship chain, and we all walked down to the fire circle. I sat between Delaney and Tammy. Maureen had her guitar out, and she led us in a song that the returning campers knew but that I hadn't heard before. It was easy to learn, though, and I joined in the second time through. The song was about wanting to linger longer at camp, and the melody was sweet and sad. By the time we'd finished singing it, I think we all had tears in our eyes. I leaned over to Delaney and asked, "Are you coming back next summer?"

"Only if you are," she said.

I smiled and wondered if maybe, just maybe, this friendship with Delaney could turn into the kind of friendship I still believed in. Maybe not the marrying-twin-brothers kind. But the close kind that lasted forever.

Eddie and the counselors gave out awards, and tonight the prizes were actual plaques instead of little slips of paper. It seemed as though everyone got one.

Kat got Outstanding Achievement in hip-hop. Annie got one for music. Brooke got one for waterskiing, and Tammy got a Sunshine award. I knew Delaney would be getting the Star Lake Cup award, and I realized I might be the only person in my cabin with no award at all.

Sami Betman came up to hand off the torch to the last Firelighter of the summer, and I thought back to that first day on the bus when Kat told me you don't win Firelighter, you earn it. I didn't understand it then. But now I thought I did. There were a hundred campers here and only four Firelighters each summer. But there must have been dozens of girls who embodied the character and spirit of Camp Star Lake. Dozens of role models. I was ready to be one of them. Maybe next year.

When Sami called out Amanda Zweig's name, I realized she was in Cabin Woods, and this was her last summer at Camp Star Lake. I cheered along with the rest of camp, and I thought, How nice for Amanda. Her last Fireside. Her last Banquet. She had probably been waiting for years to be recognized this way. So I clapped a little louder.

Finally Eddie and Nancy brought out the Star Lake Cup. Nancy said, "This year's race was quite an adventure. I'd like to congratulate all the girls who participated. The conditions were the toughest we've ever had, and you all handled yourselves well. But our winners this year are Delaney Reed and Jemma Hartman!"

It took a second for me to register what she said. Winners? Plural? Me?

"Come on!" Delaney said, jumping up and pulling me with her.

In a daze I walked up and held on to one of the handles of the huge silver trophy. Delaney took the other handle, and we held it over our heads while Maureen snapped a picture of us, and everyone cheered.

Eddie said, "We'll be engraving your names on the trophy, girls. But you'll have to come back next summer to see it. What's your team name?"

Delaney and I looked at each other. We'd never thought of a name. But then the simplest answer popped into my head. And I knew Delaney would like it. "You can just call us Friends."

Acknowledgments

With gratitude to:

- Beverly Reingold, for asking the right questions
- Carol Grannick, Jenny Meyerhoff, Ellen Reagan, and Weezie Kerr, for spurring me on with astute comments and unwavering support
- My parents, Adrienne and Neil Aaronson, for allowing me to spend my childhood summers at Camp Birch Knoll in Phelps, Wisconsin
- Gary Baier and the whole Baier family, for creating the best overnight camp in the world
- My children, Jacob, Faith, and Sammy, for their love and humor
- My husband, Alan, for making it all possible and for making every day more beautiful than the last

You are all extraordinary to me!